QVEST &
CROWN

A QVEEN WILL BE CROWNED
FIRST MVST SHE BE FOVND

MARIE SELTENRYCH

©Marie Seltenrych:

Cover design©Runaway Princesses Books

Margate, 4019

Queensland, Australia

First Printing 6 January 2021

ISBN: 9781921943362 Print Edition

©Runaway Princesses Books Australia 4019

Dedication

TO FATHERS EVERYWHERE
You are our knights in shining armour

Table of Contents:

Preface

Garty Musdo shares his most intimate desires and plans with you as he rides through the final stage of his most extraordinary mission to find a princess, invisible, missing for nigh on twenty years.

He will share his weaknesses exposed as we delve into his deepest desires and his most intimate moments. With a deep soul and a weak heart for the beautiful women he meets, he will stumble often and occasionally triumph.

Set in a time and place where knights were noted for their valiance and kings for their cruelty, Garty shares his best moments with his best friend, his horse.

Can the women he meets change his course or give him answers? Will the beautiful Chrystalina take his heart and keep it? Or will he remain smitten by Joanne and fail in his mission?

For Garty, a formidable climax looms fettered to a frivolous pageant of potential. A touch of romantic comedy ensues.

Kick off your shoes, hop into your favourite chair or cosy spot. Enjoy a wild ride with Garty Musdo and a bunch of celebrities and fly away into a better sunset. Created, edited and published by Indie Author, Marie Seltenrych. Copyrighted to runawayprincesses.com

Runaway Princesses Books, Queensland, Australia.

runawayprincesses@outlook.com

Prologue:

The town called Scatt is a last chance opportunity to redeem myself, Garty muses. He assesses the terrain and its possibilities with a new vigour and confidence.

Knight Commander Garty Musdo stiffens his robust thighs atop his glistening copper hued horse, Brill, and surveys the scene around him. He savours a deep breath of the strikingly fresh air.

Grass is longer and greener now that wintertime wanes and the early springtime weather approaches, bringing with it infrequent and refreshing light showers that soften the earth and encourage new growth in every corner of his universe.

He sighs as he dares to consider his journey thus far.

Four years and nine months ago he began this mission, searching on behalf of the King of Kallai, a wonderful country. Alas, it is still without a queen or heir to the throne.

The king is becoming impatient. The obsessed and deeply depressed king decided to call for a final escalated investigation to find his daughter.

"You must find her, for the Kingdom demands it!"

A velvet purse containing two hundred gold coins and five hundred silver coins was presented to Garty for his expenses as he bowed in respect to the King and the sword touched his shoulders lightly.

Garty knew that his emotions sometimes ran ahead of his mind, so is determined to mind his thoughts and to keep them rational.

Garty often conversed with his beloved Brill, who is his most faithful and best friend and has been his only friend over the years of this commission.

"I am sure we will find a clue about the truth of the missing princess in this town, Brill. It is now or never methinks…"

This was the 19th town he had stayed in and investigated thoroughly, thus resulting in only a smidgen of genuine information.

If the princess should not be found, the throne was imminently in danger of being taken over by the King's half-brother, Axemanix, who had been a deadly foe for years against every honourable knight or dame and especially those closest to the king. He was intent on squandering money, living in utmost luxury and treating its citizens with the hardest labour and sternest of rules that he could imagine.

Garty shrugs his broad shoulders and flicks his slightly unkempt fair hair, squints with his sea blue eyes into the distance. His ebony and gold uniform is now well worn, tottering on bedraggled. His brass chain mail vest had snapped in places, leaving only a small necklet for protection of his throat, and his mail hood was stolen a few years ago, hence he felt less secure in fighting off the marauders who hid themselves in bushes or on the forks of shady trees, and attacked at will. His soft undergarments had frayed and some precious pieces of under clothing had been washed downstream when he stayed sleeping in a woodland camp site six months ago, in autumn, just prior to winter setting in.

Chapter 1

I remember being distracted by the figure of a naked young woman bathing in the cool waters of the Bunky River. I had thought her to be a mermaid because of her glistening skin.

I did not follow her lead because my garments went missing on that fateful day. I was almost certain it was an eagle that snatched my undergarment, but concurred that its shadow manifested a humanoid. A thief, no less!

Garty had sent a written request for a new outfit but the king refused his request because, replied the king, in writing.

"Thou has not brought me the evidence requested, or any such hope for repatriation of my daughter!"

It was obvious to Garty that his ongoing personal expenses were not included in the king's statement:

"Whatever this costs, I shall fund it!"

Not only did the king refuse his genuine request, it was clear to Garty that the king was not happy with his progress. He seemed angry!

A cool wind whirls around his trunk and enters his chest with a sharp stab.

Garty's strong cool thighs hug his beloved Brill. He pats his horse's strong neck, glistening from his patient care in grooming his steed. The horse snorts lightly in appreciation.

"We have to find her anon, Brill," he whispers to his friendly horse.

Or I shall never acquire a fresh uniform and shall needs endure rags for clothing!

He shakes his head as he speaks. Hope rises again in his heart as he spies out the town. Surely good news would be his soon! He merely needs one vital clue to this puzzle of the missing princess and he will be at peace!

"This is the place everything points towards, Brill. This has to give up its secrets for 'tis the last place she may be, or otherwise we will have to break the sad news to the King that the princess is indeed lost and invisible! My heart beats formidably within my bosom, dear friend, and thou shall be with me at the end, hopefully to celebrate!"

They ride down steep rocky pathways at a good pace. He tugs the reins and stops again.

"I need a good strategy, Brill."

He waits to gain some inspiration by looking around the inroads to the town, removes his glove and extracts a map tucked in a pocket of his torn jacket.

With a small stub of charcoal, he marks the map, mumbling, "Lane to the West, church building on Easterly side, Lake Scatt towards South... and..."

The horse becomes restless taking off at a trot.

"Steady on...we will go shortly. I know, you are keen to have your feed! But I must indeed acquire the legend details..."

Garty looks around. He senses a presence.

To the left of the peak there are large boulders a little overgrown with moss.

It seems as if a shadow passes by, but he concludes it to be imaginary. However, he notices *the birds squawking and flying around the top of the largest boulder and above the oak and ash trees nearby* that sparkle with an abundance of fresh green to soothe the eye.

I shall trust my steed more readily, he muses.

"Good boy, you saw something, didn't you?

We cannot afford to lose more clothing, or our weapons, Brill. We shall be more careful now," he whispers into the horse's ear, touching his pistol near his hip, still holding the stub of charcoal, finds his weapon snug and ready.

They had left the previous town, Loopa, rather early in the morning to avoid highwaymen, who generally attacked more often later in the day because they were too drunk to rise early. However, one could never be completely sure of their whereabouts.

He continues to mark the map in his hand, keeping one eye on the boulders even as he writes every detail. He needed to perform this tedious work to keep on track, and sane!

The horse grunts and waits patiently.

They had become knitted companions, devoted to each other over the years, getting older and wiser together, or so Garty likened the relationship!

Garty folds his hand drawn map and pops it along with the charcoal stub in a small pocket, keeping his eyes peeled as he feels for the pocket. He knew exactly where each pocket was located because he had diligently and with great lack of prowess sewn more pockets into his fitted jacket despite bleeding fingers and thumb.

He then plucks the minute oligarch painting from another stitched pocket using his ungloved fingers.

"Whoever it was has vanished," he whispers to Brill.

Surely if it was a highwayman I would see crushed grasses and movement of shadows.

He looks at the picture between his fingers and thumb. It is an oil over charcoal painting of Queen Bianco, the beautiful, mother of the missing princess. The picture, now crumpled and torn on its edges, as a result of its being taken in and out of his breast pocket and compared to many beautiful women.

But none matched this beauty by a good mile, he muses. *Surely a daughter, especially a princess, might be as beautiful as her mother, even identical?*

Garty requires himself to keep this picture at the front of his mind to refocus on the invisible princess' oligarch painted depiction.

On a good bright day, like today, he can see the oil brush marks over the original drawing. *Perhaps the artist should be found as well,* he ponders? *There is no time to investigate a new line of enquiry.*

The king had convinced him that his daughter would look like her mother, the queen, the one reason Garty kept this picture close to his heart.

It is his only piece of the puzzle that I believes is genuine.

Garty is feeling exhausted this morning, having begun his day just after dawn. But, is happy to see the town close by and the prospect of rest and a hearty meal warms his heart and gives him the gusto needed to go on.

"I hear there is a great Inn in this village, called by its ancient name, but I cannot for the life of me remember what it is," he says as he notices a neglected sign made from timber with the words *Scatt* burnt on it in black lettering.

The sign has tumbled from its post and is now pointing into the grassy earth among leaves, pebbles, grass and wild flowers.

Garty feels a wave of disappointment rushing over him. He wonders just how careless the people here might be and if it is catching?

"The Maud, that's it!"

He remembers the name of the Inn.

"We will be revived after our visit no matter what happens. Let's head down into the village, and hope it is already operative for the day," he says to Brill.

With a gentle nudge to Brill's ribs, the pair make their way down the treacherous pathway towards the small town, where hewn built houses sit in a row in the village.

The hub of activity where things colloquial to the region are eventing, even as he watches from a distance.

He notices the central statue of a former king enthroned at the core of a fountain spilling sparkling water from a magnificent jug in the king's hands.

He sees smoke curling from ancient brick chimneys, blackened by smoke, debris, and birds' nests.

Miniature human figures move about, beginning a brand new day with beautiful sunshine, pausing to chat or cheer each other on, taking water from the fountain in pails and jugs as the day slips into its routine.

Gossiping, no doubt, Garty muses.

He takes pleasure in watching people interacting for a while, a trifle mesmerised at the puppet-like activity.

He had visited many towns and knew that they all kept secrets he could never uncover. His strategies would need to be hewn in a more subtle way to find out the hidden truths and myths in this town.

His mind begins to figure out what he might do to extract any pertinent information without upsetting the whole locality!

Gold is always an incentive. But, alas, my gold is becoming scant.

As the town looms closer he feels an air of expectancy stirring.

"This time, we may have good news for the King. But, if not, you, Brill and I, have tried our level best to fulfil the commission."

Perhaps I could find a homey wife and live on a country farm after that!

He laughs out loud at his own abstract thoughts.

The horse neighs as if he had read his master's mind no less!

"Don't worry, Brill, I shall not leave you even for a beautiful woman. She would need to love you as I do before I would even ask for her hand!"

More likely I would find myself locked in a damp dark basement of a tower if I fail!

His blood runs cold at that thought!

"Harder, Brill," he says, noticing the patch of smooth surface leading into the town. They rode harder for a few minutes, regressed to a trot. Brill's hoofs clinked on cobblestone. Within a few minutes he was thundering into the small town.

"We are here, Brill."

Garty pulls on the reins to slow down. He removes his charcoal grey felt hat with its gay red feather floating on top as a gesture of respect to the people meandering in the centre of town.

Folk in the genesis of their activities stop to stare at the stranger in dark leather attire, with his chain mail still sturdily harnessed around his neck, hiding his shabby undershirt. His hair glistens like gold in the morning sunlight.

Garty detects a slow pace in this town and it pleases his tired bones.

Curiosity is a colloquial trait of these townsfolk, Garty notes, as folk watch him from behind doors ajar, curtained windows and folk leaning on garden implements in pretence of rest, staring at him and his horse as if assessing his business.

"Good morning," he says in a clear voice. He greets them with a cheery wave of his hat with its red feather.

That seems to settle the mood a little. A few hands wave momentarily, then continue their relevant projects with vigour, *to impress me no doubt,* Garty assumes!

"Stop here Brill," he instructs his beloved horse, pulling on the reins to achieve a fine trot.

"The Maud Inn! Yes, the one we were told to frequent at our last stop!"

Looking around, he sees no other Inn, so surely this was the one suggested? The horse obediently trots towards a friendly looking inn painted yellow and black, with a post outside to tie up a horse and a small space for the horse to stand in the shade of a sycamore tree bursting with glints of sunshine and freshly grown bright green leaves that almost dance for joy at their early spring-birthing.

"I'll get you a nose bag, and your favourite drink," Garty says, patting Brill's neck.

The horse neighs lowly. Brill clicks his hooves on the cobbles as thought he likes the sound his master makes and orders it promptly.

"I know, you are hungry and would love a big red apple and a huge orange carrot," he says into Brill's twitching ear.

Dismounting, Garty takes note of the town main street, houses and shops, mainly taverns and stores, built in a row, with a footpath alongside for easement.

Typical town, he muses.

"Nothing changes here," he whispers to Brill before he heads up the steps.

Chapter 2

The Inn boasts three wide steps leading to an open door, painted yellow with black trims and a dab of gold paint.

He senses its welcoming mood along with the clatter of crockery and glasses, tinged with a hum of voices that carry sound waves to his auditory senses.

The yellow and black marbled entrance gives this humble inn an air of old fashioned grandeur. Carpets inlaid with emblems and designs in shades of blue, red and yellow embellish its ambience.

Clutching his felt hat, Garty stands by the entrance counter. It boasts a sign saying, "Wait here", on a mini lectern type of black and white message board, so he waits rather impatiently, drumming his fingers on its glistening mahogany. He pushes his scarlet cape behind his broad shoulders with the back of one hand, feeling this might be less intimidating for any lady who may come to serve him, or even a man servant. Garty taps on a small brass bell noticeable on the counter via his open palm. Its tone rings out like a church bell, clear and summoning. He grimaced at its sound being surprisingly loud. *At least someone should hear that!* He muses.

A homey-styled woman with ivory coloured hair tucked inside a night sky hued bonnet that flattered her moon shaped face came bustling to the desk. Garty detected the air of annoyance behind her serene facade. Her gown was darkest blue with fitted sleeves and a starched white collar. *She reminds me of a nurse I knew as a child.* He immediately feels comfortable talking to her.

He leans his flat palms on the desk and studies her face. He notes her features in order to compile his growing list of facial composite sketches. His artistic skills had rocketed alongside his ability to obtain all details of a woman's face in one momentary glance.

"Sir," she addresses Garty. "Good morning to you, Sir! May I assist you?"

She bustles about moving a small selection of items on the counter. She glances up at him with inquisitive hazel eyes with yellow flecks that remind him of a cat he once had, and a faint smile painted orange. It enhances the fashionable picture of highest quality and etiquette.

"Some water for my horse, a rosy apple and a carrot," he said immediately, beckoning towards the front where Brill patiently stood at ease tied securely. "And a little grain, if you will?"

"Certainly Sir," the woman tugged at a bell cord underneath the counter. Immediately a young woman in stable boys' olive green livery, appears, she being lost in baggy shirt turned neatly up to her elbows, and trousers tucked tightly into strong highly polished boots, came hurrying and stood before the woman. She kept her round eyes on the woman, her mistress. "Water the horse, Bubba," she orders in a calm voice with authority.

"Yes, Madam, right away," came the reply from the young female. It was almost a whisper from her tiny mouth, pink and perky as a rabbit's. The young lady bit her bottom lip with great fear and trepidation. She glances up with her wide set darkest brown eyes complimented by whitest whites, but her narrow chin was still pinned to her neck, her body as rigid as a tree covered in winter snow.

Garty notices lightly tanned skin on the back of her arms, neck and face that may contribute to her appearing older than her years? *She could be 15 or 18 years old. She is used to working outdoors.* Her hair is a shade of wet sand, tied at the back of her head by a rough ribbon of black that complete the look her employer desires. But, she has a gentle countenance about her that strikes him well. *Is she just young and shy or being bullied by the older servants,* Garty wonders? *I hope it is simply shyness for I cannot endure bullies!*

She does not look to the right or to the left as she steps swiftly outside towards his beast as a soldier might do on duty. He notices her untying the horse and leading it via a gated walkway between the inn and adjacent building. Garty watches Brill trot beside the young strapper without a murmur. Satisfied that his beast is in the best hands, he turns to the lady serving him, notices that she is wearing a badge with her name engraved upon it.

"I would like to book a room, Mrs Bouchée," he says, "for about one week," he adds. This is his usual practice, and enough time to sort out whether or not a town might yield any information about the king's missing daughter.

She smiles at the use of her name and gazes at her little book laid out before her. She pops a pair of ink blue rimmed spectacles on her nose to make her final decision. They change her appearance to one of severity, a person who refuses to tolerate nonsense! She impresses him with her demeanour and tidy appearance. *A woman who cares in particular about the latest fashion but more of good manners, tidiness, obedience and even kindness no doubt,* he thinks. *She is a woman of worth,* he muses. *I like her.*

"We can do that for you, Sir. Would the East Wing suit you? It overlooks yonder hills," she utters with a click of her tongue. Garty ponders this news for a moment before replying. He may have preferred something south-facing, to keep a look out for any highway men that might be have followed his trail, or remain lurking in pursuit of his person, or more exactly, his money. He had gained a canny way of detecting unwanted stalkers over the years and knew that his guard must always be up. However, he had no wish to cause a stir of undue fear in this woman. *Methinks the room should be quieter which might prove valuable to achieving a peaceful sleep finally. And I need to prepare a plan to extricate information from the local folk.*

"That is acceptable. And may I order meals for the duration of my stay?"

"Certainly Sir, the dining room is right here, and of course, you may have room service too!" Her eyes lift above her spectacles' rims and she stares into the centre of the room, indicating with her left hand where small tables are set with the best blue and white crockery, trimmed with finest gold, tables with small vases of flowers, freshly picked, and a small tray with condiments. High backed chairs stand proudly alongside. A middle aged man with greying hair and smart business attire, a white long sleeved shirt, brocade breast coat and tailored woollen pants in a dark tone of lead or ashes, sat alone at the far corner, quietly eating a generous heap of scrambles eggs and toasty bread, drinking tea and gazing at a newspaper spread on the table for two.

Garty wishes to be that man right now. He is famished. His mouth waters.

"We serve breakfast until 11:00 AM and Lunch will be served at 12:30PM precisely."

"I see! That sounds very convivial," Garty replies, following her eyes through the room.

"May I have your name, Sir," she says, silver pen held aloft by her finger and thumb.

"Garty Musdo," he replies promptly.

"Not the famous Knight Commander Garty Musdo?" She exclaims, her eyes popping above her glasses, as if he is a celebrity. She scrutinises his bright shoulder pads, the King's crest, three wings in a row, on two brazen pins that impress her curiosity and confirm his claim to his title.

"You have finally condescended to visit our village." She smiles quirkily and continues her rant. "It's such a shame," the woman says shaking her head. "We heard that the King has been searching for a ghost for many years now," she adds as if she is privy to the king's mind.

Expecting my agreement no doubt, Garty muses. He utters a slight cough, lowers his face before commenting in a sharper than usual tone of voice.

"Everyone may have their own opinion, but I do not." He raises his head. "I have the King's opinion and that is my reason for being here," Garty says.

Mrs Bouchée's face reddens. "My humble apologies Sir, I do not mean to be irreverent or blunt. The King of Kallai is a noble man! Of course you must carry on with your work as usual, just like me! Now, I shall show you to your room. You are welcome to order breakfast immediately!"

I smell fresh coffee, hot bread baking, and fresh apples. Aromas burst through the air and tantalised Garty's nostrils pleasantly.

Maud Bouchée closes her book and places her pen in a small crystal inkwell with a clink.

Picking up a large brass key with a label attached, she hands it to Garty with a flourish.

"Your horse will be comfortable in stables at the back. All our staff wear olive green livery, so you can identify them. We are presently designing outfits for our reception staff. The progress is ongoing. You may ask anyone for help for your beast, or for yourself, of course!"

"That is much appreciated, Madam," Garty says politely tipping his hat, swishing his scarlet cape and following Madam.

"Maud Bouchée," she says, turning her head briefly and smiling minutely, giving him her first name as privilege.

"Thank you, Mrs Maud Bouchée, I shall remember your name in my memoirs!"

She leads him through tall wooden double doors, along a corridor, through a small library and into a secluded area with a couple of doors nearby. "Number 19," she says, pausing at a door marked with a brass number. She unlocks the door with her personal key that hangs on a chain draped loosely about her bountiful waist.

The room is quite large, about 4.5 yards square, with a window nicely dressed in yellow and black floral cretonne curtains, pulled aside and tied by a golden cord to reveal the hills beyond the glaze. Below the window stands a dining table for one or two persons, hosting a polished mahogany surface with a vase atop, sporting freshly picked daffodils budding glorious yellow. Two lean-on chairs snuggle by. Garty feels that this room has a relatable ambience and might suit him well. His eyes follow the layout of the room from left to right. In the corner stands a tall polished oak wardrobe and he observes his own form in the long mirror close to the corner of the room. A bedside table with an embroidered yellow cloth upon its surface, also boasted a book shelf and below that a small cupboard door. Nearby the eye catching brass bed sports an abundance of bedding, including a beautifully woven silk bedspread in yellow and black that adds a dramatic effect by its exotic style. On the bed's far side another small table is parked, black and yellow marble with basin atop alongside a zinc bathtub boasting a fine mahogany outer sheath, just visible from this vantage point. The black silken curtain on a brass rail is curved and surrounds the bath tub, *now drawn aside in designated entry point,* Garty surmises. The toiletry area is discreetly positioned in the far corner of the room. As his eyes move across he notes a mahogany tallboy with a generous seven drawers. A fine old armchair, allocated for the weary, lingers alone in its space. Two deep blue velvet cushions decorated with embossed red and gold embroidery, lay plumped upon its sturdy arms. Next to the chair he notes a small polished oak cupboard with glass doors. Garty notices its interior holds a glass jug of sparkling liquid and two crystal glasses. A brass unlit lamp stands proudly atop the glistening wood.

"This is splendid," says Garty, genuinely impressed with his proposed accommodation. He also wonders at what cost he could stay here, but resists the notion to ask such an indiscrete question? *It will cost me most of my puny gold,* he figures. Perhaps he will end this mission with a stack of Promissory notes to repay. He inhales a deep breath and perishes the thought for the moment.

Chapter 3

"I trust you will be comfortable in this quiet corner, with a fine view outside to refresh your thoughts," Madam says, standing at the window with its floral curtains. "Our curtains are imported, not standard," she comments glibly.

"Yes, of course, that is what I thought! That is simply a beautiful view. And much appreciated!" Garty feels genuinely impressed with the ambience of his appointed living quarters.

"Help yourself to a refreshing Apple juice, made locally," Madam says, raising one arm in a broad flourish towards the cupboard, *just like a ballerina on a stage might do, Garty thinks. Perhaps she was a dancer?*

"That's very kind of you," Garty replies, taking his purse from a hidden pocket and placing a gold coin in her palm. Her eyes light up and brows rise but her voice tunes to extra sweet.

"Thank you kindly, Knight Commander. Your generosity is sublime!" She replies with a nod of her head.

"I shall settle the account as soon as necessary," he says, *wondering if he may manage it? This place seems above my budget,* he reckons. *What have I done, to stay here for a whole week?* He shudders internally.

She fingers the glistening, smooth coin and hastily plants it deep in a pocket within the tiered folds of her thickly woven dark skirts. Her bustling figure turns and silently floats smoothly through the door and disappears from his viewing. His eye tracks her sublime, vanishing movements with admiration. *She sparks a vague memory within me about a wind up doll that danced on a box a long time ago.*

He rubs his tired eyes.

Garty removes his hat and cape and places them on brass hangers inside the sparse wardrobe. The robe dangles on the floor of the space. His hat perches atop the wardrobe. He did not wish to have it crushed, so is careful to secure it safely.

Snuggling into the comfortable chair, he rearranges the cushions against his back and stretches his stiff legs, tugging his leather boots off and kicking them away from his space. Weariness rushes over him as a wave of the sea. He closes his eyes and for a few moments rests. It feels good to relax after an arduous four hours riding from the previous village, Loopa, where he had absolutely no success with his mission. Sleep had evaded him all the night before because of a noisy crowd arguing all night long. His heart sank for a moment as the thought of Scatt being the same scenario once again? He closes his eyes tightly to dissuade his thoughts.

It does feel quieter here, he thinks. *At last my mind rambles over the last days's travel through hills and dales. Rocky terrains and smooth surfaces, grass and muddy lanes, flowers of every kind come flashing back as a vivid memory to me, as if I were riding through every part again. What beautiful aromas I sense? I must eat soon!*

The olfactory aroma of primroses and steaming coffee close by dumb down his plans as he feels totally relaxed.

He wakes up suddenly! It is late morning. Garty's feet felt as though they have been bolted to the floor. He rubs his lower legs to stir circulation. He jumps up wondering where he is for a moment. A knock on his door causes him to remember the last moment before falling asleep in the most comfortable chair he ever relaxed in.

"Just a moment," he calls out to the unseen knocker. He wonders, *who on earth knows about these lodgings and who would visit me here?* He runs his hand through his thick unruly hair, and wipes his face with his palms.

"I'm coming…"

His legs are stiff from sleeping in a strange position. By the time he limps towards the door and opens it to see who is there, the caller has gone, disappeared into thin air. He pushes the door open wide and steps into the small passageway. A faint aroma that makes his mouth water reached his nostrils. He almost steps on a silver tray containing some covered dishes and a folded newspaper. He looks around but nobody is here!

"My fairy godmother, Mrs. Bouchée," he says aloud, shrugging his shoulders, then moving back inside his room with his silver tray, as an athlete might retreat with a prize. He lays the tray on top of the dining table.

His nose detects the delicious aroma beneath the silver covers on the tray. *I wonder who ordered this?* He ponders. Then he notices a small card with his name on it and the words, **With compliments, The Maud Inn.**

A pot of hot coffee tantalises his nostrils, compelling him to pour out a cup. The cup is the finest porcelain and the cutlery crafted with quality silver. He sips the coffee and feels its fine tang, awakens his senses.

"This is very good," he says aloud, nodding his head, allowing the warm liquid to baste his palate.

Ham and eggs with thick warm bread, toasted to perfection were soon devoured ravenously and his stomach satisfied at last. A small cup of apple juice makes everything absolutely complete.

"One keeps the best 'till last," Garty spoke the words as he picked up the folded newspaper. It seems surreal, even prophetic as nowhere in all his travels could he remember such fine dining in a small, unknown town, in an inn of a forgettable name? The newspaper is dated the exact date of 19 March, Year of our Lord, 1799. The cusp of a new century looms and he is hopeful that this will finally be his year of success before its demise. For the first time in years his heart leaps for joy. He grasps the stiff paper fiercely, reflecting his determination to end his mission on a high, accidentally ripping a corner containing tiny writing that he concludes is of little importance to anyone. "If one cannot read it because of its diminutive size, it is useless..." he murmurs, sighing.

His keen eye flashes through its pages as he absorbs the news about local suppliers, a farm accident involving a young family, a horse and dray. Businesses advertise their wares and preachers warn of the dangers of idle hands and the coming judgement. *An idea comes to him as he reads.*

The local gossip column is of some interest, he thinks, amused by what he reads. *The delay of eggs being delivered because of drought, fruit prices rising to a never before seen level.* Garty places the paper on the table. *I wonder if there is a means of calling the servants without rushing to reception?*

"You just pull a cord and servants arrive." As he mutters the words, he notices a cord near the wall, with a track heading through the top of the doorpost.

"Well, well, ring the bell Garty!" He says aloud, with amusement.

He tugs the black satin cord and immediately a bell rings in the hallway.

"Next step, someone must hear it and heed it," he says aloud again. He waited momentarily. A light knock on the door caused Garty to stand up with astonishment.

"It works," he says laughing as if it is a joke.

He opens the door. Before him stands a young man wearing a yellow shirt and black waistcoat. He stands still as a soldier, silently staring straight at Garty awaiting instruction.

"Well, who are you?" Says Garty, "Name?" breaking the ice.

"Droop at your service, Sir." The young man stands his ground, grinning with anticipation.

"Yes, I do need service. Here, please take this!"

Garty hands over the silver tray with a few crumbs remaining.

"It was delicious, please tell Madam," he says. "May I have a jug of wash water?"

His empty breakfast tray had a golden coin hidden under a white napkin. Garty felt light and generous and forgot that his coins were disappearing fast. With a flourish he presents the young man with a silver coin which he promptly pops into his black trouser pocket, giving Garty a huge smile.

"Thank you Sir!"

Droop returns shortly bearing a huge jug of warm water and a sparkling white towel.

"Can I get you anything else, Sir?" Droop asks Garty.

"This is sufficient, thank you, Droop," Garty replies.

The young man bows his head and dashes away silently.

Garty opens his soft leather knapsack where he transports his toiletries, including a sharp razor, face soap, and a steel comb. Following a brisk toiletry that involves washing his face, shaving and combing his hair, he is ready to meet any enemy, or to greet any friend. He tugs his boots onto his feet and reaches for his cape and hat, admiring his reflection, giving himself a nod in the mirror.

"Very well done, you handsome man!" he says gaily.

Immediately he searches for Brill, who is nibbling a nose bag happily. He has been groomed already and is keen to get to ride.

"Hey, boy, not now, later! I will just walk yonder and find a place that might help with our quest. I will be back before you know it. Just enjoy your well deserved breakfast and a rest."

From the corner of his eye he sees Bubba carrying a bucket, heading towards the chicken coop at the back of the property. She did look back for a moment but her step quickens as if she is fearful. He pats his horse again and speaks quietly.

"The little lady will look after your needs. I can see that, Brill."

Garty walks swiftly to the far side of the street, his cape flowing behind him in the morning breeze that came in soft waves from the East. The air is fresh and he sucks it in greedily. His energy is returning after such a deep sleep and now his mind is churning with ideas to bring his mission to a satisfying and triumphant finish.

The printer's name is written in black and white lettering above the door of a three storey building, unusually high for a small town. "Jael Newspaper" Garty reads the words above the door, *just like a newspaper,* he muses in jest. He pushes open the wooden door that is slightly ajar into the foyer area. A small front desk is before Garty, where a man with grey hair is busily writing on a large piece of paper. Wearing silver rimmed spectacles, he looks above them at his first visitor for the day.

"You need something?" he asks in a brusk tone that declares he is very busy.

Garty tips his hat and stands near the desk, slowly retrieving the oligarch picture from his breast pocket.

"I need your help," he says smartly.

"You want something advertised?" The man looks up.

Garty notes his name on the desk, and then speaks.

"Yes, Jael, I do. This picture with words beside it!"

Garty places the little painted scrap on the counter.

"Now, can I have your name and whereabouts?" Jael bent his head and began to write as Garty gave the information required.

"How many copies of your newspaper do you distribute?"

Garty makes this inquiry as a logical one.

Jael looks up. He is not used to interrogations of this kind.

"This is a town, not a city!" He snaps. Then Jael looks as if he is about to send Garty away on the spot. "However, we have passers by, like yourself, who take our product for many miles to other towns, so I cannot give you an exact count, but possibly one hundred folk read this paper daily!" Jael says this authoritatively.

"That is quite a good number, considering there seem to be only around fifty folk in the town, and so many may not read at all!" Garty says, immediately regretting his words.

Chapter 4

Jael looks fiercely into Garty's eyes, with thunder looming within his soul. His countenance changes quickly, and he is completely self-controlled again.

"All news is not read in papers. Some is read in eyes," Jael adds smartly. "Word of mouth is also powerful." Jael adds, as he advises Garty, with his eyebrows popping automatically.

"You are correct Mr Jael. I will trust you with this painting." Garty said this with a little concern. The picture had never left his possession in almost five years.

"This is not very printable," Jael says, picking up the little painting and scrutinising it.

"It may not turn out as you wish." Jael says shaking his head vigorously.

"Can you touch it up then? I can pay you," Garty says laying two shiny gold coins on the desk, hoping for success.

"I notice you are very artistic…" Garty adds, indicating the drawings on the desk near Jael's elbow and the special pen standing in a superior brass and crystal inkwell filled with black ink. Garty spots a twinkle in Jael's eyes and is hoping for approval and success.

"It's possible," says Jael, picking up the coins, pulling out a drawer and placing them inside, closing the small drawer. He then picks up a key from a tray and locks the drawer.

"One cannot tell if thieves might be watching," he says, glancing out of the window to the street.

"I understand." Garty said, searching through the window for a sign of thieves. He sees nobody out there at the moment.

"Now, these are the words I need to be alongside the picture."

He dictates the words to Jael.

Jael writes them down precisely as Garty says the words, using his superior pen.

"This will appear in tomorrow's news," he says. "And if you want to place it there for longer than a day, it will cost more," he adds.

Garty dips in his purse to find another two coins. He placed them on the counter.

"Four days, is that enough?"

Jael nods his head.

"That's enough to cover the cost of calligraphy, art, posting and advertising, with all your own words copied precisely, errors and omissions excepted."

He stares at Garty to get his final approval.

"Of course! Thank you Mr Jael." Garty smiles and continues. "I shall return to collect the original painting on Friday, if I may?"

"That will be suitable for our joint purpose," Jael replies amicably. "I will keep it in your file." He reaches for a large manilla envelope on a shelf behind his desk and places the notes and painting inside, with all details intact. He seals it with a warm wax seal that Garty earlier noticed on a wax burner sitting upon a second shelf behind the desk.

Garty feels greatly satisfied and leaves the building. He already savours its success!

This may be my last town and stopover? His wishes are ardent in this matter. *Surely this advertisement is the linchpin?* Garty decides.

Before he returns to the Maud Inn, Garty pauses to visit to the local cobbler a few doors from Jael's Newspaper office. Everything is conveniently located, Garty notes, enjoying the short walk and fresh air, with aromas of apples cooking, ink from printing, and camphor Laurel burning. Together with a fresh breeze, flowering trees and an abundance of spring buds popping their heads. Every house has a small garden in front and this made for a paradisiacal ambience that Garty loved. *I could live here for ever,* he thought. Garty strides through the open doors of Cob's Shoes. He looks towards the sunlit corner on the easterly facing side of the workshop. Smells of fresh polish, burning rubber and boiled coffee beans erupt in Garty's nostrils.

Every corner of this town has its distinctive smells, he cogitates deeply.

"Good morning," greets a young man with sandy coloured hair and blackish grey eyes glancing at him from his cobbler's last where he is hammering studs into a sole with gusto.

"How are you today, Sir? What can I shoe for you?"

He laughs and Garty laughs with him.

"You shoe can do something," replies Garty. They laugh again for a moment, bonding over their personal, silly little jokes. He decides to add another pun and continue this frivolous laugh party. "I am well heeled, thank you," Garty informs, thinking *what an enjoyable personality this young person has.*

"You must be Cob?"

"Hah, well said. I am Cob!" the lad replies, reaching out to shake Garty's hand. Firstly wiping his palm on his woollen, grey jacket, leaving a shadowy mark.

"Garty" says Garty as he reciprocates the welcome hand. Firstly removing his leather and mail glove, exposing pale fingers.

They should be friends forever, both thought. Their eyes say it all as their souls collide in merriment.

"I need some new soles, and a few stitches for my boots," Garty explains, removing his feathered cap and pushing his cape behind his shoulders as he stands before the workbench of the cobbler.

"Soles and stitches are our business, so this happens to be your lucky day! Just a moment," the cobbler says, as he removes the tan leather shoe from the last and places it by another shoe on a shelf. As he turns again towards Garty, he mumbles an excuse. "Otherwise I should not know my left from my right." He tilts his head left and right as he utters the words. "Heel and toe are never mixed up in my head!"

"I might ask for a dance but my shoes are killing me," Garty replies. They laugh again. Everything they say seems funny!

Garty then removes one boot and places the long leather object on the workbench counter, feeling positive about this experience.

"This boot is in a bad state of decay. Not well-heeled as you suppose, Garty!"

Garty nods. They laugh again.

"I am certainly not well heeled, or toed for that matter," Garty says. His heart beat a little faster as he wonders whether banter and laughter is the trade mark of Cob? He had met jovial people before and he did not have complete trust in their abilities. *This man should be a jester for the king, he muses, not a cobbler, unless his cobbling is superior to another?*

Cob tossed the boot in his hands like a piece of dough being kneaded for a pizza oven, or a meatball from offal, with expert accuracy and speed. *He is clearly experienced in boot mending,* Garty thinks, feeling relief swish over his thoughts like a wave of the sea. For once in his life, his doubts are confounded and completely incorrect. *This is a good cobbler for sure!* Witnessed by his dexterity in handling a boot as easily as forming a meatball without superior meat. Garty decides that, *these boots are literally dead meat that need a superior fix! Oh no! He wants me to leave them here! Or to make a new pair!* His toes curled at this prospect.

"Time for new boots, methinks," he adds, looking into Garty's eyes and seriously admonishing him without words. "A time to buy and say bye-bye?" Cob says seriously.

Garty's heart drops. He struggles with this idea for a moment before replying. He loves his comfortable boots and wishes to repair them for one hundred years if possible. Now that his money is almost vaporised, he struggles with the thought of not only losing his boots but being barefoot for a season. Or even one day! And who would give him a new pair, certainly not the king!

"I cannot afford a new pair of boots right now. Could you make an exception and try to repair them today?" He removes the second boot as he speaks, sitting on a complimentary wooden chair, sprinkled with shades of polish, provided for those who wait.

The young cobbler looks kindly at Garty. *He could be a king, or the son of a king*, Garty notes his demeanour with reverence.

"You seem like a genuine person, you have honest eyes," Cobb tells Garty.

He can obviously read faces, Garty thinks. *He's a kindred spirit!* His interest in the face of a princess had quadrupled over the years and the picture in his pocket was imbedded into his mind at last. Garty wonders *does this man knows something about the kidnapped princess, or does his interest only pivot around feet?*

"What are you trying to say, exactly?" Asks Garty, becoming slightly frustrated momentarily. *Of course I am honest! Occasionally, I have slipped up without bad intentions!* A naked women passed through his visual cortex. He shakes the image away as his hair flicks too.

"I am thinking of loaning you another pair of boots until I can do a good job on these," he says following a moment's silent thought.

"I have a rather large foot," Garty says, bringing his foot into view, standing on one leg. "Big Foot could be my middle name."

Garty removes his big foot from the counter and measures each foot against the other. *One may be bigger than the other,* he reckons, wiggling his toes sticking out from holes in his black knitted socks.

Cob gives him a surprising answer that he would not have dreamt about.

"Big Foot, or big feet, Garty, I have some rather large boots right here, practically made for someone with a large foot," says Cob, bringing out a fine, shining pair of knee high boots from underneath the counter.

Garty steps back in awe!

"These were made for a tall general who never returned, sadly," he adds. "Nobody has collected them in ten years, so I guess they are not needed. I have heard that he may have expired and gone through the vale." He drums his fingers on the counter as his blackish grey eyes stare into Garty's now misty focal features.

Garty is taking his words in and trying to withhold his feelings bubbling wildly.

Chapter 5

Can this be a dream coming true?

For so long now his dreams had turned to nightmares and he is now extremely cautious about feelings of gaiety, even mild feelings.

"They are flexible, yet firm, great quality. One cannot procure such a quality product these days. Quality has diminished with too many players in the cobbling business. Please try them on, if you will, Mr Big Foot," he adds happily. Garty senses his friendship and wants these boots more than anything now!

Garty reaches over and picks up the tanned pair of boots slowly, amazed at what he notes as boots fit for someone of a much grander and higher position than himself. Exquisitely designed and made for comfort, he notes, almost aghast at their beauty. He gingerly shoves his right foot into one and tugs the leather into place around his calf.

"Hmmm, not a bad fit indeed!"

He stamps on the floor for a few seconds, wanting to dance with happiness. "Maybe I should learn to dance," he adds, twirling around. "Let me try the second boot, Cob," he says to the cobbler. Now he feels more joyous than he has done for months, and simply because of the most luxurious pair of boots that he could not afford in a million years!

"Perhaps you should join a circus?" Cob says.

They laugh for a long time. *It is such an absurd idea,* Garty thinks; but, *totally amusing,* Cob thinks.

He presents him with the second boot as though it is a sword on a red velvet cushion, precious, worthy of a Knight.

Garty tries it on. He marches upon the shop floor for a few moments, peering down at these new boots. The leather is smooth as a silk cloth and strong as the skin of a dragon.

"If I had loads of gold I may be tempted to buy them, but today it is not possible for me to do so. I must also return my old boots to the king shortly," he says slowly as his facial features appear downcast.

"I hear that you are on the king's business, so I understand completely, or very well. You shall use these boots for a time, without cost, and when you return, bring them back and I shall give thee thy boots repaired. Hopefully the leather will not tear as it has become very thin in parts." He is shaking his head as he studies Garty's old worn boots. "But for you, my friend, I shall do my utmost so that you do not part with your boots this week."

Garty happily leaves his name and connection to the inn nearby, signing a promissory note to release the loaned boots, floating rather than walking on air by the exhilarating experience.

"I shall walk faster now," he says jovially to the cobbler, whose eyes pierce him and then his smile widens. They shake hands with sincerity and part ways.

Garty walks along the crude pathway that becomes smooth at one particular area. He looks up from watching his new boots in a mesmerised way; there before him is **Scatt Bank.** He desperately needs to withdraw more money, however, he knows that his account is terminally low. A lady on a shopping spree, wearing a bright velvet bonnet with a sweet face catches his attention. He almost runs her down being distracted by his boots and the Bank Sign on a brass plaque.

"Sorry Madam," he tips his hat and bows somewhat as an apology.

The woman acknowledges his apology by a faint smile and movement of her lips and eyes. Her eyes are darkest brown, Garty notices, feeling his face flush pink. No words are uttered from her lips. Garty takes a good look at her face for one moment, a flash second, as he has learned to do to avoid intimidating folk. He is continually on the lookout for the king's daughter, despite the fact that he has not spotted anyone exactly like the queen in the painting he carries. He now begins to wonder if someone like this picture exists or what if she may look different? Immediately he dismissed that notion. He will be faithful to the King until she is found if only in his thoughts, he determines, walking on air with his new boots. *I love this place, he decides*. Sadly there is also a sign on the bank's front door.

"Closed! That is just my luck!" Garty mutters. He decides to return another day. His funds were not completely dissipated and he will sign promissory notes if he needs to do so.

Garty's next stop is to the barber shop, where he is greeted with a warm welcome.

"Sit down and relax," says the barber, Mr Trink, who noticed Garty as he enters through the ajar door. Mr Trink is alone, humming a tune, waiting for the day's surge in customers and he is excited to see Garty, knowing already that he is on the king's business.

Word travels like stormy winds in these parts, Garty muses, snuggling in the great big chair with arms and a firm cushion made with finest black cow leather. Trink's tools of trade are set out like a doctor performing the most intricate surgery. Little pots of ingredients, stubby brushes, blades all shimmering and sharp lay waiting for usage dormant in a neat row. In a warming oven nearby Garty can smell the aroma of hot coals and smoking warm towels, white, fluffy and ready for use. A convolution of mirrors, some with handles to enable holding, lay on a small table covered with a fine linen woven white cloth. Everything in this realm gave one the feeling of order and efficiency, and anticipation of a great experience, even a spiritual one. Garty can barely wait to experience some calming touches and refreshment for his aching body and soul.

"So, would you like a shave and a hair cut?" Trink asks, reaching into the warm oven, flicking a warm towel and placing it on Garty's face, carefully avoiding his eyes.

"Mmm," Garty moans in ecstasy. He nods his head. His personal grooming has become less frequent and his tools of trade are somewhat on a lower grade level than Trink's superior sharp razors, scissors and combs.

Trink, as a magician weaving a magic spell, spins a full body sheet over Garty and tucks it around his neck, being careful not to make it too tight and frighten his client into leaving abruptly. Garty does not stir. He is a fearless man because he has become so, primarily from his experiences for almost five years on the king's quest, avoiding highwaymen, thugs, cheats and flattery until today.

Now is a time to relax and recoup my manhood to its former glory, or something like its former glory, Garty muses tiredly.

Just as he begins to fall into a stupor of delight, he remembers why he has come here to this town and his soul awakens vexedly. I must find out what I can or this work will never end, he reminds himself as Trink's droning voice hovers over his chair and he feels his breath near his temples, crisp and clean like the sheet over his hurting body? *Soon I shall be in a trance if I am not alert,* he reminds himself. Arguing with his inner man, he rebukes his desire for pampering and deep rest. Bed was the place for resting and he would do that later, when the day was done. He reminds himself of the four poster bed with its plump pillows and silk covers waiting his pleasure, and is satisfied with his plan.

As Trink paints his face with luxurious oil, Garty's mind meanders and he finds himself thinking about what steps he has taken to find the missing princess. He is sure that he covered every possible piece of ground that might have been involved thus far.

As Trink bathed his face in sweet warm lather, Garty's thought wandered to the hidden things he had uncovered over the years, the possibility of a crib being involved, and children being found abandoned in some towns? To date nothing had checked out as a definitive, but there was a new possibility of truth in this town and he was determined to find it.

Once enlightened by his inner thoughts, Garty's detective mind began to churn with questions. Garty decides to ask the barber for any information he might have known about the missing princess. The business had been in the district for twenty years. Garty hoped earnestly that something may have been said about the situation over the many years and he could glean the clues he needed to end this saga.

As the sharpened blade gently touched his sideburn area, Garty relaxed a little. Trink was still talking about beards and faces and skin, so Garty felt there might be an opportunity to tilt the subject to his princess quest.

"Some men love their beards so much they never stop missing them..." Trink says, in his hushed deep tones related a story about a local man and his emotional connection with his beard. How he felt colder without his beard... Garty listened quietly under his sharp razor waiting for an opportune moment to question Trink.

"He really missed his beard and could not wait for it to grow again...Which fortunately it did!" Trink rinsed his blade in the bowl of icy cold water for a moment.

The word *missed* gave Garty his moment for questions.

"Have you had many folk talking about the missing princess?" Garty bravely asks Trink as he now resharpened his razor on a honing strop for a smoother finish.

"Well, it is strange but from where I came, there was certainly plenty of talk a long time ago. But, of course, nobody has seen or heard of this child in many years. Sadly, these events occur and the persons involved go underground and usually the victims are never seen again." He says this in a voice of authority gained by ageing well.

He began the warming and shaving process once again, smoothing out Garty's taut skin to a silken feel.

"You will soon be softer than a baby's bottom!" He says this triumphantly. "Thanks to my splendid techniques."

He sounded very satisfied with the results even before he is finished. Garth takes a mental note. *A proud man no doubt.*

"Mmm, nice, it feels just like a newborn, wonderfully calming," Garty muttered. "So, what is your opinion Mr Trink? Do you feel there is more to this story about the princess newborn?" Garty dares ask this question and risks a rebuke if his timing is not precise.

"I will help you in this project," he said at last. Garth breathes a sigh and waits in anticipation.

Trink still held the sharpened blade close to Garty's neck, causing a slight tension underneath the sheet and towels. Finally he spoke proudly again.

"Not many people around here know something about me, and my connection with Gypsies," Trink says, tension in his voice causing his tone to reduce greatly. Garty has to listen intently to hear his words now. *He must know something I don't know,* he cogitates excitedly. Garty's attention is stirred to a frenzied pitch underneath the sheet and towels. "Stay really still Sir," Trink commands.

Garty obeys.

"Please, say on," he says to Trink, popping open his eyes in a moment of excitement. *Perhaps this is the moment in time when the mystery shall finally be solved. Was Trink involved? Why did people not know about his background?*

Garty wonders about this gypsy story, and his mind starts buzzing about how *gypsies being involved* was a nice slice of truth to note in his book. *It is a sound possibility that I have not investigated until now!*

Trink begins to tell his story, slowly, thoughtfully.

"You see, I was with the traveling folk for many years as a boy and teenager. They were my family..." He pauses to let a slice of his personal information pie be digested by Garty.

Garty waits with his mouth open as if ready to swallow a big piece of pie.

"Keep your mouth closed during this process, and keep still," Trink directs Garty.

Garty is barely able to contain his bodily pose and wishes Trink would tell him more and rapidly also. He even thought about stopping the whole shaving process and meeting with Trink at another time today, to have a more in-depth conversation. His mind buzzed like a bee over a fresh bloom. Had he finally found the right connection to the crime? *Maybe lunchtime would suit better than this busy time of day?*

"You know these people?" Garty asks, looking into Trink's disturbed eyes, with eyebrows furled and mouth set as a peg in the ground.

"Relax Mr Garty, please, otherwise you may have scars and look like a highwayman not a gentleman." Trink said jovially.

"And no respected person wants that!"

Garty tries to relax again, taking a deep breath and closing his eyes once more.

"Gypsies know things," Trink says with definition. "Gypsies know something about all this, for sure!" Trink says seriously.

"Not my family, no we would never do anything criminal. We do what we have to do, but not criminal. Never!"

He is so adamant that he almost slices Garty's countenance with his sharp blade giving him a real scar. He pauses to compose his thoughts.

"Twenty years ago now, something happened that caused a lot of bother! Let me see?"

He gazed away as if looking into the past in a crystal ball for a moment, and then continued.

"We had been in this building for a few years I remember and we were still using old fashioned implements, like the huge long razors and rough towels. Now we have upgraded of course."

Chapter 6

"These gypsies you mention, do you know anything about their travels? Or family name? That would prove helpful to me, and the King."

"Let me think about that," Trink says.

"I am sure I can remember something of interest for you. I would like to help," he adds.

The men are silent for a few minutes as Trink finishes his shaving process, placed a fresh towel over his face and massaged Garty's face as if he is a small child. Garty feels loved. He then removes the towel and places it in a space designated on the nearby bench for used towels.

Without asking, Trink places a hand mirror in front of him. "What do you think, friend?"

Garty tilts his chin and turns his face right and left and is happy with the results. He wants to feel the skin but his hands are still trapped behind the large sheet.

Later, as Garty gazes at every angle of his tidy hair, Trink says, "I remember now. 'Kiano,' that was the name of a family involved in something suspicious about a baby. A newborn!"

As Garty reached into his purse to extract gold coins a customer arrived through the door.

They greeted each other.

"Morning Wallop," Trink said cheerily. "Please take a seat."

Wallop, a middle aged man with unkempt grey hair and a "skunk" stubble, sits down to wait for Mr Trink's attention.

Mr Trink passes a newspaper into his hands and the man nods thanks, taking the paper and staring into its pages. He then turns back to his finished client, Garty, who has stepped aside and waits to pay for the service. He notices how quickly Trink reacts in keeping his customers happy. He feels a warm familiarity with this man and admires his precision and care. *A man of impeccable taste,* Garty reasons in his mind. *I shall offer him a goodly sum.*

"Thank you Sir for your custom," he addresses Garty, who hands him three coins.

"That is more than sufficient!" he says, giving a slight bow. He extracts a couple of silver coins from a tin box with loose change and hands it to Garty, who shakes his head, refusing this offer politely.

"I believe you deserve what I paid and the change can be yours to keep or spend at you wish!"

Garty felt good saying this.

"Very well, thank you, Sir!" Trink spoke in a whisper as though this was a most private conversation as he pops the coins in his small steel box and locks it swiftly, placing it underneath the desk. "If you even need my services again, I shall be very happy to help."

"Thank you so much," Garty replies.

He plants his hat on his head.

"My cape, if you will, please."

Garty cannot reach it from this position and Mr Trink immediately comprehends his dilemma. He steps away and reaches to the brass hanger, then passes the cape to Garty, bidding him good day with a massive smile beneath his fabulously tempered moustache.

On his short walk back to the Inn, Garty decides to check his notes over the years regarding gypsies being involved in the kidnapping. His own doubts about this aspect of the kidnapping came to the surface.

If gypsies had kidnapped a child, why do so? What could they gain for their community?

Their motives were certainly not clear to him. But, there was some involvement by gypsies, of that he felt certain now, and would pursue that line of thought in this very town. *'Kiano' is the gypsy tribal name I must remember,* he vows.

Following the footpath he again feels sleepy, and the new boots he had been loaned by Cob are beginning to tire his feet already. Even after a hearty breakfast he is hungry and ready to eat once again. He hurries to the Maud hoping for a great feed and to write down more notes for his project.

Mrs Bouchée has prepared a hearty lunch of freshly baked bread, local fish from the river running near the town of Scatt, and greens grown in the lower valley. Of course there was also the complimentary apple drink, a famous local product. She reserves a table in the centre of the room for his dining pleasure that boasts a perfect view of any person coming or going into the Maud Inn, which is satisfactory.

Removing his boots later in his room, Garty sits with his long list of notes that he had been taking over the years. They were contained in a ledger that was quickly being filled with extra bits of paper and numerous notes in pen on every page. He now also had hundreds of quick sketches to compare to the picture of the queen in the oligarchy. *That is becoming more confusing over time,* he muses. Nothing had struck him in all these years about anyone he had met, and a wave of despair flooded over his mind as it had done many times in the present year.

He lays down on the bed and is soon drifting away. He enjoys an afternoon nap and is ready for a clean up and evening meal by 5:00 pm. He visits his horse Brill, who is enjoying rest as well, and the best of care. Garty pats his horse's neck.

"This will prove a very rewarding exercise in this town. I feel certain about that!" he tells his horse confidentially.

"You need to feel the breeze in your mane, Brill, I can see that, old boy. I am sorry that you have had to wait. Tomorrow we will go for an earnest ride," he whispers into his faithful beast's ear that wiggled in response.

Garty noticed that Brill sports new shoes as well. The *Farrier has been busy, methinks.*

"That makes two of us, Brill. See, these are only borrowed, but yours are permanent until they wear out!" *Another bill to pay!*

He feels the burden of a horse shoe debt and subsequent bill even as he tries to be cheery for his horse's sake. "I am happy for you, Brill." He needed to count his money again and to find some way to gaining more cash. He heads to his room to do just that immediately.

The velvet bag felt a lot lighter these days and Garty knows he will need to visit the bank again before the week was out and ask for an overdraft. Bills were mounting up in this resort style inn, and *Mrs. Bouchée will not take any Promissory notes,* of that he is almost certain. Garty rubs his forehead and closes his eyes for an instant. Already he smells the evening meals' aromas floating through the cracks in his door and gaps in the windows.

"Well, tomorrow is another day. I shall rethink everything then!"

He hears a bell and closes the shining brass buttons on his breast jacket. His hair and face looked respectable. *The barber has done a magnificent job,* he muses. "You are a handsome fellow," he says aloud with a grin, staring into the mirror at his slick reflection. It is then he notices a shadow passing by the window in its reflection, but reminds himself not to become paranoid. After all, there are quite a number of young servants in the establishment.

"It must have been one of them," he mutters to confirm his thoughts, closing his door carefully and locking it with the key. He was not going to take any risks.

Having enjoyed a hearty crusty vegetable pie with delicious apple crumble for dessert, Garty took one of the complimentary newspapers, returned to his room, removed his outer garments and snuggled into his comfortable chair to read the local stories.

Some time later he reached for the eiderdown on the bed and covered himself in the chair without missing a snore.

Garty awoke to a loud knocking on his door. For a moment he wonders what has happened. He throws off the eiderdown, stretching to move his body parts. He pulls the curtain open. The sun has not yet risen, so what is going on? How long has he slept? Hastily he throws his cape over his shabby woollen undergarment and bare chest. He opens the door gingerly.

"What's the problem?" He asks Droop, the young servant in livery standing at his door.

"The problem, Sir? Mrs Bouchée says you are to come to the foyer at once. People are waiting for you."

"Of course. Tell her I shall come speedily."

Garty quickly pulls his breeches and boots on, and slicks his hair into shape. He rushes out the door, but remembers to lock it as well. He pops the key ring onto his leather belt around his waist next to his trusty pistol.

He pauses in his tracks when he nears the reception room. The night lamp is still lit. In the subtle light he is shocked to see that the room is filled with people talking, about twenty in total. Mrs Bouchée is standing at the front desk, taking names and offering drinks to those with cash to spend.

"There you are Mr Garty! About time! These people are all waiting to see you."

"Whatever for?" He asks this even though he has a grave suspicion about what they really want!

She picks up the newspaper and holds it towards his face.

"This is why," she points to the word, "reward..." and read the rest of the sentence under a printed picture of the Queen, "is offered for information leading to locating missing princess."

She puts the newspaper down on her shiny surface.

"See what you've done, Sir?" Her lips are tight and her eyes brilliant with dismay.

She looks splendidly angry, Garty notes with a slight tinge of fear. He knows that she is a feisty woman, and now he must convince her that this is not his intention.

"I am deeply apologetic and I thank you for your capable care of the situation."

"We can manage, but it's unexpected," she adds staring at Garty just like a Mother Superior in an orphanage he remembers, and cringes before this woman.

"Surely this must be good for business?" Garty argues. He sees that business is ongoing with the patrons drinking apple juice, coffee and milky drinks. Along with slices of baked apple pie and crisp pastries.

Mrs Bouchée makes a noise that sounds like a gurgling in her throat.

"Not if they are thieves and robbers! How can I control what they do or where they wander? There are too many!" She is speaking clearly now.

Garty backs away a smidgen.

"Please, do not worry. I will take care of everything," Garty says.

He moves to the centre of the dining room.

"Please, ladies and gentlemen, I will have an interview with each one of you, but you must keep order in this respectable establishment."

He looks around to see how he may manage the impending surge of people.

"I shall sit here, at this table, Mrs Bouchée. If you will, please take each person's name and whereabouts, as you are efficient in this area," he said across the heads and pairs of eyes, aiming towards Mrs Bouchée at reception.

She seems relieved in a fashion and strode into her role of being his organiser. Coming from behind the desk, she moves with grace and takes command of everyone present with her powerful voice.

"Everyone, please take a seat outside as there is a long bench there. Also, those who arrived first can come into a line here," she indicates her reception area and stamps her foot to indicate the spot.

A buzz erupts in the room as folk note who was here first and second, and so on. Everyone seems to know who was there before another, which is a great boon for the present situation. Within a few minutes a line has formed of four persons near reception and a few folk standing near the door, to indicate that they were here quite early. Others head outside and are seated in the early morning sun that begins to spread its warmth and light across the hills and into the valley majestically.

Chapter 7

Mrs Bouchée asks for paper and pens to be dispersed to Mr Garty, who sets up the interviewing chair and table at arms distance from everyone else waiting. Everybody can see but not hear what is going on.

Garty feels in his pocket for his velvet purse. He wonders if it is to become light as a feather, even empty in the ensuing hours of interviewing. Dandy, a trainee waiter comes across to Garty.

"For you, Sir," says the young man in black waistcoat, trousers and yellow long sleeved shirt, the standard service uniform." He holds a silver tray with coffee, apple juice and toasted fresh bread with melting butter and some honey.

"Thank you, Dandy," says Garty, reading his engraved name tag. *Another addition to my bill,* Garty notes in his methodical mind.

Before he begins eating, Garty beckons for the first person to come over and share her information quietly. Everybody's eyes follow her process. This is not how he wants the interviews to progress. He smiles and nods at the folk staring at him to indicate that he can see them too. They immediately look elsewhere, *a little embarrassed,* Garty reckons.

"Mrs Bouchée, is it possible to give all these people a hot drink and some of your wonderful bread and honey?" He stares as he speaks, so she will hear him. She is staring straight at him now, listening carefully, he notes.

Immediately he makes a generous gesture, "I shall fit the bill, be assured of that," he adds, wondering *how on earth am I going to do so, but I am determined.* Miracles did happen around him from time to time, and he desperately needed one this week!

A happy buzz erupts and then silence as Mrs Bouchée gazes at the crowd. She has never had to cater for so many folk in this town since the great flood twenty years ago. Her lips are dry and her heart pumps speedily but she gathers her wits about her.

For this moment she was born, ponders Garty!

"Certainly, Sir Garty Mudso Commander," she says in a halting voice, choosing her words carefully.

"Staff, please bring hot drinks or apple juice to everyone here. Please add everything to the Knight Commander's account at his bidding!"

"Here, take one of these pieces of bread," he offers the first woman who sits on the wooden chair with its velvety padding. Gladly, she takes up the offer. "Take the apple juice too," he pleads, while he sips hot, dark strong coffee.

I need the boost to my energy, and this drink is superb.

The woman slurps her juice as if she is parched with thirst. She smacks her lips and smiles, showing gaps in her front teeth. He knows that many folk may have had nought to eat that day, so considers his gesture a necessary service to the town. To gain information, Garty knows deep down the folk must be well fed, not fed up. He has learned this lesson recently and applies it to this very day.

"Thank you for turning up. I appreciate anything you can tell me relating to this mystery," he says, waiting for her to wipe her lips.

She leans forward and he can smell her breath, fresh apple juice and other aromas he was not familiar with. He does not flinch! Determination has taken him thus far and he was still adamant in seeking the truth! For years he had endured so much that it was impossible to comprehend all the misinformation around the country.

The woman seems relaxed and relates information about voices she heard in the woods in the month the child disappeared.

Garty faithfully writes everything down and records her particulars too. He quickly makes a brief sketch next to her information, noting *her eyes are dark brown, sun kissed skin, long angular features, high forehead, cows lick hairline on her temple, auburn hair, some greying.*

She watches him intently, loving every moment of her fame and the small fortune he slips into her long, bony hand, partly covered in a black fingerless glove.

And so the queue of folk progresses, each one in their own time and with their individual confidential information.

By lunch time Garty is exhausted and wishes that he had never offered a reward for information. He had distributed over twenty silver coins and knew Mrs Bouchée would require a dozen gold coins to pay for her servants and service.

Lunch was a relief but short lived. Mrs Bouchée personally came to his table and presented Garty with fresh bread and home made jam.

Garty could smell the aroma of the bakers in the kitchen baking bread non stop.

Mrs Bouchée insisted that he take a break of fifteen minutes to refresh.

Garty took the time out as he did feel his head was spinning.

He exits the room and pops in to see how Brill is faring in the stables. Brill nudges Garty and seems happy enough.

"I know, you want to take a ride into the hills and let your hair fly," he says, patting the horse on its fine strong neck, feeling its sensitivity to his touch. Fodder and water are close by, so it is clear that his horse is being well watered and fed.

He is just a little restless, Garty feels.

"Maybe tomorrow," he promises. "But we shall see," he adds in case more informants turns up and folk gather again in order to reap a reward. *What a fool he was,* he thought. *I should never have had the word 'reward' printed. Why didn't I learn faster?*

He questioned everything he had been doing over the years and felt disappointment with his own progress again.

I am a dismal failure!

He walks back from the barns through the laneway at the side of the establishment and takes stock of the entrance to the inn where people are still milling about, sitting on bench seats, drinking apple juice in porcelain beakers, swilling tea and thick brown coffee in tiny cups. *Mrs Bouchée's best presentation crockery fit for royalty is on display. How much could one of these cups cost me?*

He had worried that she might have sent all the folk packing for fear of thieving and fighting eruption in her domicile. About ten people are waiting to be interviewed. He tips his hat and settles down to proceed. And so the afternoon progressed.

At the end of the day he looks up to see if anyone else is waiting. The place seems almost deserted. Mrs Bouchée and a couple of helpers are busily cleaning up dishes with a clatter now that the hoard has departed to their homes.

Whilst gathering his notes, he notices a dark shadow near the door of the building. Just a glimpse in the window and then *a figure in the open doorway glides cautiously into the room*, he notes.

His guard shot up in case this may be a robbery. The person glides forward. *She is like a china doll gliding on a smooth surface.*

A woman wearing a black veil over her face, black gloves and a black shawl and long skirt with black boots, barely cobbled stands before him, trembling.

This is rather odd.

Garty holds his breath and rests his thump on his pistol hidden on his hip as he looks into a darkened face, shielded by her black and ornate lace covering.

He moves his hand to the mahogany desk, relieved.

Beyond the veil he sees her troubled soul. His heart melts momentarily with compassion.

She may be in dire need of financial assistance, a widow perhaps.

But, she does not attempt to sit down. She glances around briefly and then moves closer, looming over his space.

Garty looks into her eyes and waits. His eyelids feel heavy.

Is she hypnotising me? I must stay calm!

She barely says anything, much to his chagrin. He holds a coin between his fingers with his other hand. He listened intently as her hand moves alongside her lips to keep her words very private.

"Tomorrow, noon," mysterious black eyes dart one hundred and eighty degrees and back to Garty's gaze. Her lips are pursed. He can work that out between intricately woven patterns shielding her face. She presses something underneath his fingertips that touched his pistol butt a moment before. Before he may ask anything of her, she turns and with head bowed low, exits the Inn. Garty still has the silver coin between his forefinger and thumb.

"Well, I never saw that coming!" He murmurs in a whisper. *She gave me something and took nothing?* Questions jump into his mind immediately. *Who is this woman?* He did not get her name or address.

Does she have a vital clue that I cannot yet fathom? What will happen at twelve noon tomorrow?

"That's it then?" Mrs Bouchée says, marching towards his table to remove his used dishes, cups and plate. "Clean up time at last," she mutters as she smiles briefly, an unusual thing for her to do.

Relieved to see the heels of his last visitor no doubt, he reasons. He could definitely agree with that sentiment!

"Thank you, Mrs Bouchée," Garty says, rising, weariness flooding his veins. He shuffles the many pieces of paper and piles them as neatly as possible. He would now have to revise and check all bits of information no matter how large or small, and decide what would help in his quest. The small piece of paper with a map drawn in blackest charcoal lay underneath his thumb. He had no idea what it was all about.

"You go and refresh. Supper will be ready in about one hour," Mrs Bouchée said. He noticed beads of perspiration on her crinkled forehead and appreciated her more. It seems that he was her special project. Her face beams with joy as the many visitors had been happy to spend their reward in her establishment. Some even booked a night at the inn.

"Business is booming," she repeated over and over again, and boasted that she was a good businesswoman who could detect a golden moment and capitalise on it!

Garty had overheard her voice in high tones expressing her prowess in hospitality in the kitchen, out of his sight, but not of hearing. It made his heart burst with gladness for her wellbeing and success. Her cash register was filled with silver and gold coins and other monies, he noticed as she slipped another couple of coins into the safest place. Garty knew that she would make sure that most of the money was locked in her strong safe before nightfall.

God Bless her! He thought as he left the room. Back in his quarters, Garty stares at the little piece of paper with the charcoal drawn map. He lit the lamp to inspect it more closely. An X marked one corner, a few 'v' shapes along with a squiggly line.

What on earth is this map about? Is my life on the line? Is this a cryptic warning for me?

He felt so tired as he stared at the small grubby piece that he moved to sit in the most comfortable chair and almost dozed off immediately. Jumping up pronto, his stomach churned with annoyance at his sleepiness. His inner man spoke sharply to his drifting thoughts. He determined to be more alert and investigate all possibilities before his commission and job were in jeopardy!

Now is not the opportune time to be sleeping on the job, he muses wryly. He snatched the jug of water near the basin and splashed some on his face, drying it with the fresh towel supplied. He awakened his senses somewhat. Looking at his damp image in the mirror, he spoke these words, "That's better. Wake up man!"

He strolled around the well watered yard, smelling a glorious aroma of apples that made his mouth water as he passed by Mrs Bouchée's flourishing apple trees.

Swiftly, he plucked a fine blushing pink apple and tucked it into his trouser pocket, feeling somewhat like a thief in a garden. But, nobody saw him, so taking a last breath of the invigorating aroma, he took a new route. He walked swiftly towards the stables sighting a young man in livery. He was diligently sweeping the floor of the stables. He was tall, extremely thin and his smile was a knockout. With hair that fell onto his face when he moved, Garty imagined his own youth being like this young lad, innocent and garish, awkward and full of life's expectancies.

Weariness would not come near him at this age, he mused with a tinge of jealousy over his lost youth.

He loitered nearby, thinking about the message in his fingers. The young man stares at him with a quizzical expression. Garty reaches out his big, manly right hand to the young man, "Garty Musdo on the King's service."

The young man almost bows to the floor. "Ted Bingy," he says. "Pleased to meet you, Sir." He wipes his hand on the side of his baggy olive green breeches and holds it out for Garty. Following a manly handshake, Ted leaned both hands across each other on the tip of his broom handle and waited for Garty to continue the conversation.

Chapter 8

"Are you a local?" Garty asked tentatively.

"Born and raised here, beyond those hills," he says in a happy tone, pointing in an easterly direction.

"Good, that's good news! You may be able to help me now. Could I trouble you for information about the area you lived in?" Garty asked politely. The young man wiped his hands on his trousers again and licked his lips furtively.

He must be thirsty, Garty reckoned, *or uneasy.*

"Would you like to come into my quarters and take a drink?" He asked.

The young man shook his head vigorously.

"Not allowed Sir," he says determinedly. His eyes shift from left to right as if searching for someone or something?

Garty observes that *this young man is desperately trying to behave according to rules set by his employer. Or, maybe something else is wrong,* he wondered, *like a threat?*

"Well, that's all right, Ted," Garty says. "I would never consider upsetting you. But, I was wondering if you can help me for a moment?" He holds the charcoal map aloft for Ted to see clearly. "This little map with the X. Can you say if it may be a map of the area or is it something else?"

Ted turned the piece of paper three hundred and sixty degrees.

"It's upside down, Sir. If you look at it this way, you can see the hills and the winding road. It is a map of this region, that's clear to me! That's just a few miles from here, over yon way," he pointed in the direction of the long road that Garty had traversed a few days ago.

"Hunty's Dale," he says recalling the name of the specific area. Garty takes note in his mind.

"There is a sign like an X somewhere up there, on the cusp of the corner. It may be overgrown now," he adds, for clarity. "It's been a while since I traveled that way. The rolling hills are just along the way."

Garty detects a lull in his voice, and he waits a moment to comment.

"Can you show me the best way to get there for someone new to the area?" Garty asks as if he might be a tourist visiting, which in fact was almost correct.

"I can! If one follows Hunty's Dale for around four miles, you should come to a clearing near a wood. You see the little strokes here, that's the wood." He hands the map back to Garty.

"I hadn't noticed the strokes! That is very enlightening. I appreciate your help."

He crosses Ted's palm with a coin, and Ted beams. *He clearly was not expecting that*, Garty notes.

"Any time, Sir. I'll tell you anything you need to know." He moves away and continues sweeping vigorously. "I need to get on with this job before sunset," he explains, raising his eyes briefly underneath the shade of his baggy cap.

"Certainly," Garty replies. "Carry on!" Garty turned towards where Brill was waiting to see his master.

"I will see my horse for a few moments, if you permit?"

"Yes, indeed! I am finished doing his stall. Lovely beast, your horse," he adds, happily sweeping away from Garty, ensuring no dust particles irritated his eyes.

Garty appreciated his kindness.

"Much obliged."

Garty patted his horse who nuzzled into his hand gently. He was happy but Garty could sense that he needed a long fast run to keep his muscular frame in tip top shape. Riding together for years Garty felt his mood through a touch of his hand on his faithful friend's muzzle.

"Tomorrow, dear friend, we will ride!"

Garty says, gazing as the sun sank lowly and the long shadows came hurriedly across the town, bringing in nightfall.

Garty produced his surprise, a round, pink and golden apple, wiping it on his sleeve, holding it in his palm. Brill had no hesitation in picking up the apple with his big mouth open and his teeth flashing. Garty rubbed the saliva of his horse on its neck, patting him as he did so. The horse grunted with joy. "Now, it's time for me to eat. We shall meet again tomorrow, dear friend."

Garty left and followed the aroma of sweet and savoury flavours. He sniffed deeply and said lowly, "What has Mrs Bouchée cooked up for supper?" He hurried to the dining room to get the answer and dine in style as usual.

Early the next day, Garty was laying on his bed when he heard a loud knock. He groaned. More people must have turned up for a reward. He still had not waded through all the scribbled pieces of information he had gained from thirty or so persons in the past day. Now it was on again. He rued the day he had placed the word "reward" in the local newspaper once more. Ignoring his feelings, he called out, "Hold on, I'm coming."

He has already partly dressed and was laying with his chest bare. Quickly he pulls on his only shirt. It was a dismal yellow from age, having lost its fresh newness long ago. Holes and small tears had formed on weakest areas such as under the arms and near its cuffs.

Garty made a promise to give it a wash in his bathtub tonight, and try to repair it with a needle and thread, but now he had a lot of work to do, presumably.

He opened his door and there was Mrs Bouchée herself, carrying a tray of fresh bread, coffee in her favourite silver pot, and a large jug of her freshest apple juice.

"I see you are up already, like the birds," she adds.

She likes early risers, Garty noticed.

"You are an astonishing woman," Garty replies, feeling special that she had come personally to bring him this sustenance. "Yes, I did wake up early. It is a beautiful morning, fresh and inviting," he says thoughtfully.

"They are already waiting in the dining room and a few outside. So, you had better get on your horse and ride, Mr Garty," she adds with a smile he noticed was permanently on her face for the last few days. "Contrary to my beliefs, these folk are honest and more than willing to spend their reward on my establishment, so I am happy to refresh their bodies as their needs arise." She paused, and then continued. "But, for how long I can keep up with this noise and frantic process, God only knows, for I am sure to be wearing out shortly?"

"Mrs Bouchée, I am so happy that you have been more than gracious to me and the townsfolk. I have this idea…" Garty paused and took the tray from Mrs Bouchée's lagging arms. He placed it atop the cupboard with the lamp and turned back to the figure standing in the doorway.

"I concocted a sign to be placed in the front of your establishment."

He picked up a piece of yellow parchment that he had found in the room. It said:

"To Patrons: Please note, there will be no more rewards for information necessary from 12:00 noon today! Thank you for your co-operation! Signed: Garty Musdo!"

Mrs Bouchée takes a deep breath. She is bobbing her head, so Garty feels optimistic as he waits for her utterance.

"Yes, I think that is a fine message for everyone. We can all relax after that, with a nice jug of apple juice. I have this new recipe including cinnamon on my agenda."

"I can't wait to try your cocktail creation," Garty says, bowing as Mrs Bouchée turned and Garty closed the door behind her.

"I shall post this at the front..." his words echoed behind her skirt folds and fine leather shoes as she hurried back to her reception post.

Shortly after his breakfast was consumed, Garty posted the message in front of the inn. Those waiting became quite agitated and scorned at him. Some read the words aloud for those who could not read.

"Look, it says there will be no reward for information from twelve midday! What does this mean? Is our word not good enough?" One woman with long brown hair and sharp features shouts loudly.

"Yesterday, they was paid for words and information. Now, we shall get nought...!" She seemed to be gathering support as the people nearby nodded their heads and murmured against this notice.

This is not going to go down smoothly, Garty thought as he felt the surge of people around him with vexed-faced! His heart beats inside him like a Grandfather clock pendulum and he could not stand any more of these comments. It had seemed like a good idea to stop the crowds forming and so many turning up to gain a gold or silver coin, of which he had nearly 'zilch' remaining.

He turns to the little group waiting outside reading the poster.

"Good day friends, I'm Garty Musdo," he says to the group who stared into his eyes with mean expressions, as if to say, "Who do you think you are denying us fair payment?"

Garty detected their inner mood and wished to change that promptly before things became nasty.

"You are, of course, exempt as you were not advised, and have been waiting already..." he says graciously, swinging his cape behind him and bowing, with eyes locked on the group so they did not move a hair.

His forehead feels as if a tight bandana strangles his thoughts. He feels trickles of perspiration on his temple hairline. That settled them down momentarily and their conversations buzz with a happier tone. He relaxes for a moment and sighs as he beckons the first person waiting in the queue to come and give their information. He has his little bag of coins in his pocket, so that nobody dare steal anything without his being acutely aware of it.

By mid morning, he had finished speaking to the final informer, Jobe, a farmer who gave him information about a baby crying in bygone times. Garty resists the urge to dismiss the man entirely.

The idea of a baby crying in the distance was something that occurred everywhere around here with many children coming into the world continually. There was *always the possibility that this cry was from a baby princess*. Even though he persuaded himself that *this may be so*, he also doubts the whole story.

"Thank you for taking the trouble and time to inform me of this instance." Garty placed a silver coin in his palm and closed his ledger.

He rises and shakes the man's hand, who swiftly puts the coin in his purse and says goodbye with a flourish.

Garty feels the meagre contents of his velvet bag now being in stark demise. He has perhaps five or six coins remaining, which would not suffice for his bill for accommodation, let alone all the food he has been plied with by Mrs Bouchée. He knows that *she shall be subtly demanding in receiving her dues.* He groans and reminds himself to *visit the bank and to seek an overdraft* for he was surely becoming bereft of cold hard cash.

Having taken his notes to his room and placing them in a stern box with a key lock, he hides the box in what he deems to be a safe place. Then he slicks his hair, washes his face and is ready to visit the bank manager, minus an appointment. He already knows this will cause some delay, but nevertheless, he has to do this, he decides. And *the quicker the better*, he reprimands his procrastination.

Walking along the cobbled pathway towards the bank, Garty stares at the ground. Now deep in thought and wondering if *this may prove a vain exercise?*

Chapter 9

What shall he do if the Bank Manager refuses his request? He hears a few, "Good Days" and tips his hat, although he had no interest in any conversations right now. His pocket was getting so long now that he is rummaging on the bottom of the bag, finding balls of fabric under his nails. His heart pumps speedily and he wishes he had not taken on this project five years ago. He is simply *a king's fool!* Before he knows it, he almost walks into the sign hanging outside the bank.

Crafted in glorious mahogany wood and Gold, a fitting sign for a place to keep ones' precious treasures swings with the words 'Scatt Bank', and no 'closed' sign. He sighs and takes a deep breath. He pushes open the heavy dark mahogany door with its brass lock. He reads another sign with the words, **'Open'** on its door in parchment held by a chain, hook and door stopper.

He removes his hat and looks around. The highly polished marble on its floor signifies a grand place, *a place of perfect safety*. Behind bars on his right and left are bank tellers, waiting and working diligently. He walks to the empty spot where an aged man, with greying hair and thick glasses, glares up to stare at Garty, multitasking even as he held pieces of parchment and a rubber stamp in his hands. He continues his work as Garty waits - as though his present occupation is of the utmost urgency!

Garty steps back to wait, his boots making a clinking sound as he stepped, *a lone customer in the room that echoes when he walks*, he muses about himself, and he feels a little embarrassed. The ceiling is high, with lamps hanging that swung when he opened the main door. It feels quite cold inside the building, somewhat of a surprise to Garty. The facia of the bank seemed to hide its surprising interior. An oil painting of a famous person called "Huckleberry Clove" wearing a multitude of badges and stars glared at him from the wall. Garty cannot help noticing a similarity between this iconic hero and the man with the stamp behind bars.

That man could be his father, Garty notes nonchalantly.

"Sir, can I be of assistance?" The man spoke from behind bars that gave him some protection from any enemy wanting to take others' monies and treasures.

Garty steps forward, his heart racing. He knows that his *chances of gaining an overdraft are slim*, but he must try.

"Yes, Sir, I wish to see the manager," he says.

"I am the manager!"

Garty noticed the name "Jammy Clove" on a plaque nearby.

"Certainly, Mr Clove," said Garty quickly. He must *make friends with this man* before he gets thrown out! Garty smiled as best he could.

"Come into my office and reveal your business," said Mr Clove rising from his seat. Garty watched him as he hobbled towards the end of the counter. "In here!"

He beckoned Garty to a door on the side marked with the label: **Manager**. Garty followed Jammy into a small room with a desk, two wooden chairs, a book shelf, and a safe with a huge brass lock.

"Take a seat," he instructs Garty. "Would you like to reveal your business here today?"

He slipped a sheet of parchment from a small locked drawer and a black pen from a stand in order to write the details. "Would you like to open an account? Borrow money? We are here to help you," Jammy said politely.

Garty wondered: *why does he used the pronoun 'we' when he is clearly alone? Is someone else spying on them?*

Garty braced his stealth. He is now about to ask him for money, a lot of money and his emotions bubble over with anxiety.

"Yes, I would like," Garty says in a rush. "To borrow money, please!"

The man looks up.

"Give me your personal details, name?"

"Garty Musdo!"

Jammy's face lit up as a lamp newly lit and happily burning.

"Well, not Knight Commander Garty Musdo, on the King's business?"

"The same," replies Garty, accepting the manager's hand in greeting. *Now this is different,*

Garty thought. *How did he find out about me? Of course, it must be from the newspaper*, he assumes.

"How much would you like?" Jammy looked up and into Garty's eyes, testing his resolve.

Garty is keen to get as much as possible, but does not wish to appear greedy.

"Fifty gold coins and one hundred silver coins," he said after a moment's thought. He had already deemed what may be necessary to finish this mission whether it was a success or not, and his expenses for the final phase of his mission coming quickly to an end. If he did not use all monies, he could simply put it back into the bank account.

Jammy stopped moving and is quiet with his thoughts. Garty wonders if he is about to hand him a refusal?

He wrote the amount on the parchment in front of his bony hand, then waves the back of his hand towards Garty, signalling him to leave the room. Garty looks at him in dismay. His heart feels like a stone flung on the waters of life.

"I need to open the safe," he says abruptly, as a way of explanation, rising from his chair without grace, holding tightly to the dusty desk.

"May I assist?" Garty asks shyly, not knowing if this is the right or wrong suggestion. Jammy's eyes flew at Garty in anger and Garty stepped away as much as he could in the tight space behind him.

"No!" Jammy almost shouts.

"Sorry Mr Clove! I shall leave thee in peace," Garty said quickly. *How foolish I am to offer help in opening a bank's safe?* Garty arose, took his hat in his hand and stepped outside the manager's door. He looked around. There are three customers at the counters now.

Each one smiles when he looks their way.

A young woman and her chaperone, an older lady wearing a servant's cap, and another gentleman in business attire who wears a well trimmed black moustache and a black top hat. They all seem to know him, thought he could not remember meeting any of these people. *Friends of friends of mine*, no doubt, he concludes.

"Musdo, you can come back in!"

He hears the manager's gruff voice calling from the office. He is seated. A pistol and a small bag lay on his desk. Garty is not shocked as he often held his pistol closely especially where money was involved.

"Sit down."

Garty seats himself in the allocated chair. He waits for the manager to speak.

"I always keep my pistol ready when handling valuables."

Garty understands and nods his head slowly, with his eyes fixed on Jammy's eyes. He knows that being face to face with a pistol holding person, the rule was always *'move nice and slowly'*!

He slid the intriguing sealed purse with its tiny brass lock and wax royal seal toward Garty and a piece of parchment that he had written upon. "Sign the form to say you received the amount you requested."

No questions asked? Garty, elated, takes the pen and signs the form at the bottom X. He slides it back towards Jammy. He is already calculating his next financial move, *pay Mrs Bouchée!*

"Take it. It is yours," Jammy says without flinching. "You already signed the promissory declaration. We expect you to abide by this agreement!" Jammy Clove placed the pen in its holder rises wearily from the chair.

"Thank you," Garty says.

He reaches ever so slowly for the money and withholds a gasp as he holds the little purse close to his heart. He wants to say, "I got it" and jump around, but stays completely still. He is not out of the building yet!

"Come back any time you are in trouble." Mr Clove said this without emotion. He stands awkwardly again, shuffling around his chair as if it is infected with wormwood, then walks around his desk to open the exit door.

Garty watches Jammy Clove with fascination as he waits to engage the simple rule of politeness, a short bow. With hat in hand and money in heart, he exits the open door feeling like a stage actor departing a scene into the wings, not looking back, waiting for applause.

Garty walks on air back to the inn, exceedingly relieved of his major worry, cash in hand! A fuzzy feeling of gratitude comes over his brain and without warning tears flood his cornea. He brushes them from his eyes and attributes this phenomena to the rising wind blowing from the East. He pats Brill on the way to his room. He finds the side entrance more private and chooses to use that way to exit and enter his quarters. Closing the door behind him, then locking it, removing his cape and hat, he finally relaxes.

He breaks the seal and opens the small lock with its attached brass key. He lays the contents on the purse on the small dining table, moving the vase with fresh flowers towards the back side, near the embossed green and gold papered wall that serves to bring an austere atmosphere to the room.

Separating the gold from the silver coins, he places half of the total sum in his velvet purse. He shall *pay Mrs Bouchée for her services anon*, he decides immediately. A tap on the door indicated that lunch is served, so Garty quickly places the rest of the coins back in the purse they were delivered to him, folding down its leather catch and locking its brass lock. Placing it deep inside a plain looking tin box in the table drawer, but with a small lock. He takes the keys and pops them in his trouser pockets. Feeling content with this process, he focusses on his appearance for a moment. Running his metal comb through his hair, he is satisfied. He then splashes his face with water, dries his hands and face and for a few moments stretches to his full height.

Mrs Bouchée's delicious luncheon awaits, he tells his image in the long mirror, feeling humbled by her attentiveness and care of himself as though he was a king. He liked it very much. She had pre-arranged that it was served sharply at 11:00 AM, at his request due to his appointment at midday. He estimated a ride of approximately twenty minutes to reach Hunty's Dale, the X on the little note. His feels a surge of energy and excitement as his life roller coasts along today. It is simply a successful day thus far and he intends to enjoy a brisk ride with Brill.

Thanking Mrs Bouchée, who is busier than ever in the kitchen, he bows at the doorway when he spies her form. She acknowledges his gratitude with a tilt of her fine head, under her neat baker's cap. He heads off to his room to collect his cape and hat and catch up with his faithful steed, Brill, who is waiting in anticipation of a momentous ride.

Garty notices that Brill is well watered and fed. He sees Bubba striding towards the chickens with a feed bucket. She has a faint smile for him but quickly bows her head and hurries to her work. Garty knows that it is she who cares for Brill. He motions a friendly thanks with his hands but she does not look back for any acclaim. He also sees Ted turning to smile at him and hurry away towards the piggery. *What well orchestrated servants Mrs Bouchée has,* Garty notes mechanically. *I am grateful to them all,* he muses as he strokes Brill's neck.

Placing the saddle on Brill's sturdy body, Garty thinks about some of the information snippets he received, trying to recall *a silver spoon with an engraved date on it? Could it be the date the princess was born? It was one possibility,* he reasons, setting the bridle on Brill, ensuring everything is nicely secure. He places his rifle in a special slot alongside the saddle by his hands, and ensures that his pistol rests securely near his ribs.

"One never knows who will greet me today?" he whispers into Brill's flicking ear. He neighs lowly.

Chapter 10

"You are always ready, true friend," he says patting the thickened hair on Brill's long neck again. Brill pranced in anticipation of a nice long ride into the distance where he was happiest.

Garty wants to ensure that as few people as possible see his departure or where he is headed, so he exits through the side gate that leads into a seldom used laneway. From there he works his way around the hills and towards the spot marked with an X, near a wood in a small clearing. Even from a distance he sees smoke coming from a semi-circular shaped roof of a caravan. He instinctively knows that *this is the right place* and feels grateful to Ted for his information.

Settling Brill near a fine crop of grass beneath the shade of a sycamore tree, he dismounts and heads to the highly ornate van, decorated with gold and red flowers that seemed to match his cape brilliantly. He feels strangely at home as he passes by a couple of piebald ponies and calls out to see if anybody is home.

"Hello there," he shouts.

A face appears in the small window draped in the finest hand crafted lace. Immediately he recognised the woman who summoned him at the inn. He notices her name above the door, **'Janda Clairvoyant'** in carved letters.

"Come in Sir, this way," she says pushing open a creaky door butted against steps at the front of the caravan.

"Thank you, Janda." He says these words nice and loudly, so that she heard her name.

Garty bounces up the steps, ducks his head to avoid collision with the top door jamb and finds himself safely inside. A hand reaches behind him to shut the door. Her angry face is now uncovered and her black veil lays casually on her shoulders. She is wearing a finely embroidered dress made with purest white linen. *Not bad for a pauper,* Garty thinks, wondering *from whom she did steal the fabric? Or did she create the fabric? Can she be the one who had the child in her grip,* he wonders? Now, however, *she is a possible informant,* so he makes sure to be on his best behaviour.

"Sit down, here," she indicates a crafter chair with engravings of angels and demons. Its well worn seat glistening from the best bottoms sliding onto it.

"Thank you, Janda," Garty replies, squeezing into the narrow chair and placing his cape over its back. He removes his hat and places it on the clover shaped table near his elbow. The woman is seated opposite. She pauses to glare into his face for a moment, *so* he keeps his mind vacant *just in case she can read minds,* he muses. He waits for her to speak first, a courtesy that she appreciates.

"I told ye that I would divulge information regarding a baby I have seen in the district."

Garty nods and waits again. "Say on," he says. He wants her to hurry up, but she seems to be gathering her thoughts continually.

She is working out what to say and what to leave out, no doubt, he thought. *That is fair enough,* he feels.

"What I saw that night I can clearly recall. It happened on the heath and there was great clapping and dancing because of the goods the marauders had taken from the castle itself. They were screaming and jousting for a very long time.

We waited until they settled down, mostly to a drunken sleep."

She looks up from her thoughtful pose.

He wonders that she did not *consult the crystal ball* he sees on a shelf behind her head. But, he said nought.

"I'll get thee a drink, Sir," she says, rising and taking a jug from a cupboard. She fills two little cups with a fine golden liquid.

"Apple cider," she explains, sitting down again, slurping the drink noisily. Garty slurped his sup in response and respect.

"One of our clan managed to get hold of a most beautiful box, shaped like a giant egg."

Well, Garty's thoughts rang like a bell.

Why had he not heard about this in all his travels? Her vocals drop lower as secrets unfurl from her scarlet lips.

He leans closer to hear. He sees the whites of her eyes. She responds with a warning stare.

"Yes, it was an egg?" he says, nodding his head. She is happy to see his attentiveness, unhappy at his nearness. She inhales loudly.

"It was not an egg, but a marvellous jewel studded crib with split opening. Custom made!"

Garty ponders this description of a crib.

An egg is a crib?

He tries to visualise the object of discussion in vain. She sees his curious expression and immediately smacks the table.

"I knew it. I shall have to show thee," she declares, as though it was the Magna Carta, and not a baby crib! She wipes her nose as she bumbles through the caravan, then bends down on the floor, emits a huge groan and rises up again, holding an object shaped like an egg with its shell split on top. It is a disappointing shabby linen cloth covered frame.

"This is the one. The actual crib they borrowed from the marauders, those evil thieves," she says with great expressions of disgust.

He examines the crib delicately. It has a bamboo shell and the cloth is worn so much in places it is transparent. He also notices that some objects perhaps as large as buttons have been ripped off, leaving small holes and loose threads all over its frame. He manipulates the creaking twin tops that join at top centre. A little gap remained so that a hand could pull either hood down. He is quite impressed with its design and engineering properties.

This could well be a special crib if it was covered in a kaleidoscope of jewels.

"It looks like a very unusual crib," he says, handing the delicate object back to its present owner. He wants to take it with him, but refrains from asking being aware of tensions surrounding him. "So what's the story you wish to share about this crib?" He asks with sincerity, so that *she may not shout at me for any misunderstanding.*

"It was so beautiful, everyone's eyes lit up when they saw it. Of course they had to take it away hurriedly. Over time the jewels were shared by the members of the tribe."

She says this with misty eyes.

Garty feels convinced this is true. But, he wanted to know about its contents too. And if this family were surnamed Kiano?

"What about the child?" Garty asks slowly, as though it is not urgent.

Her eyes light up like a globe. She shakes her head vigorously as if trying to sweep it away. "She was a good baby, so sleepy and quiet that nobody knew she was inside."

Was the child dead already he wondered? Did they kill her? His blood turned cold at his own thoughts. He waited for the gypsy woman to continue her story.

"When we found her, we were flabbergasted. It was a serious crime, we all felt that way. We would never steal a little one, just the jewels, I suppose, in line with our Gypsy code!" She grins eerily and her teeth, filled with gold fillings flash before Garty's frozen face.

"Where is she?" Garty asks without emotion. His mind and physical composure are now at odds. He needs to know the outcome of this tiny child, treated recklessly for her exquisite crib.

The woman shakes her head and shrugs her shoulders. "I have no idea, nor does anybody else!"

So that is that. Everyone knows what happened twenty years ago but not today. I have wasted my day and my time, he thought, groaning with sudden weariness at his own failings for a vulnerable human being.

"But I know where we took her," she says in a hushed tone. She leans so heavily on the table with its three legs that it shakes with her vehemence. She draws her veil partly over her face, *hiding her bitter emotions*, Garty assumes.

"Please tell me more," Garty says, dumbing down his flailing exuberance.

"The orphanage, that's where she was left, wrapped in a special scarlet shawl, the poor little darling. It broke my heart..." She stops as her emotions surge quickly.

Was she actually involved in this kidnapping and disposal of a child? Garty takes mental notes. He restrains his distain. Smiling artificially, he stares into her half-hidden face and he notes fear flashing through her eyes.

"There now, do not be troubled by your thoughts. Which orphanage?" He adds this question quickly.

That is the clue that could perhaps determine the final outcome of this quest.

"There, over there," she says, waving her arms towards the woods beyond. She searches her mind for the name of the orphanage. "Grave...no, Graceful, that's the name, I think. The place is gone to wrack and ruin now. She was there!"

Garty is both disturbed and excited about this revelation. The woman rises and hurries towards the little window, peeping through the curtains using a strong word that Garty ignores. She turns back towards Garty and despite her veil he can see that her face is ashen, as if she has seen a ghost.

"Get out quickly. They followed you!" Her tone is one of anger and dismay. "Quickly, this way," she wiggles past the table and tugs on a rolled up tapestry on the end wall, allowing it to flop down, showing a tapestry of horses and riders. She pushes open a small door behind the scene. The door swings open, revealing a small platform outside. "Now!" She speaks with urgency.

Garty almost forgets his hat. He doubles up and crawls through the small open door, *designed for children no doubt,* he muses as he twists and turns to bring his shoulders through. The woman speaks quite sharply to someone he did not know was below the doorway.

"Crystalina, get Snow and Mr Garty out of here, quickly. They are coming yonder!" Her tone is snappy.

Garty, for the first time, sees a figure hunched over a loom. At first he thinks *it is an old woman.* She turns her face towards him, flicking her long hair.

"Yes, Mother," Crystalina replies dutifully.

His heart almost stops when he sees the creature before him, placing her loom on hold and rising up from a three legged stool.

Her eyes are so beautiful, like two crystal balls in one face. He can barely believe his own eyes. *Mother must be the old gypsy woman,* he reasons, but his mind is confused, ecstatic and broken in one look from this young woman. Her hair glistens in the sunlight. It appeared as dark as night and as bright as sapphire and amethyst united as one. She is sleek, not very tall and her figure is superb, delightful to his eyes. His face turns pink with his own thoughts of delight. *How can this miracle happen to a grouchy, introverted and crazy woman I have spent a good hour of my time, listening to her meandering?*

"Come on Sir, quickly now, we are waiting."

He hears her voice and it sounds like music to his ears. He shakes his thoughts as if they are snow flakes and stares at first, totally unable to think clearly. He simply gazes at her in awe. She is now seated on a white horse fit for a princess with its golden mane flowing in the gentle breeze. Exuding confidence, she sits bareback, with Brill next to her. Garty is shocked that she has no saddle, no whip, no lead, yet she is totally in charge of this horse and his own steed.

His eyes mist over and he wonders if he is dreaming. He must wake up before they are all captured! With that thought in mind, Garty leaps from the small balcony, instantly takes the reins, grasps the pommel, locks his left foot in the iron stirrup, and mounts Brill, pressing his hat firmly on his head, flicking his cape towards the horses's rump. His desire soars to impress this Empress of horses, flaunting imperil of his life or reputation for a ride alongside.

Crystalina is already hugging her horse, Snow, around its neck, and her black satin hair tie has fallen on the ground. Her body is leaning forward and he can just see an outline of her perky rump, round as a robin's breast and strong as a young horse's rump. Glistening blue-black hair flows behind her as the silken veil of her noviciate. Her voice is husky-sweet and demanding.

"Ride low and fast, Mr Garty," she orders him in a guttural voice that seemed to emit from an alien.

How does she know my name? She is a genius, he moans, heaving a huge breath. He almost faints with excitement as his thoughts rush to and fro. *Ride low*, he repeats *and fast*, he adds, repeating her sumptuous words to his soul. His heart cannot respond but beats faster and faster as if it is rocketing to the moon.

"They will shoot," she adds for clarity. "They are killers!" She shouts this time! "Faster!" Snow, her horse bolts! She hangs on like a circus act, thrilling and courageous.

No time for fear now, Garty thinks, somehow jubilant, yet dismayed at the unknown possibilities.

He rides like the wind and she rides as a whirlwind! Brill must keep up with a fine white stallion with hair the colour of clouds and so wild he is magnificent.

Brill is up for it and loves every minute. Fifteen minutes of hard riding sees them go through a thicket.

Chapter 11

"Stay low and slow," Crystalina says, throwing her head back towards Garty, whose horse is on Snow's heels. They arrive at a clearing and the sound of a bubbling brook causes Brill to neigh lightly as if speaking a 'thank you' to the stallion who has now stopped and is prancing lightly after the long run and snorting happily.

Crystalina turns towards Garty and slips off Snow's back as easily as sliding a slim foot into a fine slipper. His heart tumbles again. Everything she does fascinates him. Her flowing scarlet dress, decorated with the most intricate embroidery and fitted to perfection on her young and slightly voluptuous-virginal frame, stuns his thoughts more than he can bear. He wants to rush to her, sweep her up and kiss her strawberry red lips, nuzzle in her silk tresses and gaze into her spell-binding eyes. Instead, he jumps off Brill and leads him to the stream for a well earned drink of pure mountain water. He dares not to look at Crystalina, *for I might morph into a jelly man.* He smiles at his own thoughts.

She has brought Snow towards the stream and is now sitting down on a flat rock almost overgrown with moss. He glances at her and it happens again, his heart fibrillates wildly. If he is not careful his emotions will get him into serious trouble with such a female of extraordinary strength, dexterity and of course, immense beauty. He knows that he must take more control over his emotions but it seems impossible right now! Crystalina is casual and unaware of her affect on his deepest thoughts, his disturbed psyche. She looks towards him and her face is grave. He waits for her to speak to command him to kiss her. He will, gladly. Instead, he chokes on his words and allows them to spill out as a dribbling tap.

"Who are these people tracking me? Do you know?" He genuinely feels disturbed and disappointed with himself for not noticing anyone following from the inn. He was careful, so how did they know where he had gone?

"These people are enemies of King Swanfeather. They are known as Axemanix's hit men! They must have followed you. It is your fault entirely!" she says with daggers in her eyes. He genuinely experiences a shower of fear raging through his torso.

"I am so sorry," he says. "I never meant to cause any trouble to you and your mother."

"They know us and have threatened us before," she says slowly. "Very dangerous people." She pauses.

Her thoughts become private for a few moments.

"Do you want to drink or carry on?" She asks in a factual tone.

"Carry on?" He asks. "I thought we were safe now?"

"No, Sir, we are not safe. I must hide out somewhere near here for a while. You must go back to the inn and stay in safety," she adds. "I am worried for your safety!"

Garty tosses his cape back behind his shoulders and shows the butt of his pistol.

"I am armed," he says proudly. "And I can shoot well," he affirms.

"All very well, but there are three of them," she argues logically. "I observed them coming." She pauses and appears distressed momentarily. "They will take Snow for sure, and maybe me too, if they feel they need a hostage," she says gloomily, but then she smiles and smashes his heart again.

Garty wants to take her in his arms and make passionate love to her, right here in the soft green grass and luscious daisies, primroses and cowslips, roll around in her arms for the rest of his life. He mentally rejects his thoughts and speaks as a rational being and not a love maniac.

"I am sorry to put your lives in danger. I shall take your advice and return for now."

She steps towards him and he quivers inside. Of course, he has not paid her mother. Did she want money? He slips out his velvet pouch and shakes out two gold coins. *That is equal to a month's wages, maybe a year's wages for some*, he reckons. *I owe this to her and her mother.*

"Please give these to your mother?"

Crystalina holds her palm out and he places the coins within, accidentally touching her firm skin.

Every part of this young wild woman was firm and flexible, soft and firm, incomprehensible to his soul. She shattered his every thought and her power slithers deeply into his soul, mind and body.

She must never know of my feelings. I am, after all, a Knight and gentleman first and last.

"Whatever my mother said to you, do not believe her. She is a great liar." Her words are almost spat out, as if hatred lives deep inside them. She tosses her hair and her eyes beam into his, piercing his heart and shattering it into a million pieces. He literally shakes his thoughts as a dog shakes water off its coat.

Garty is shocked at her words. She obeys her mother but now says she is a liar! This is a female that he cannot fathom!

"Please, give this one to your mother, for I gave her nothing at all after she came to see me yesterday. Please promise!" He hands her another golden coin. His eyes plead with her crystal ball eyes that now turn dark and broody. Crystalina snatches the coin roughly, scratching his palm slightly. A shiver races through his spine. She has become angered. She controls herself and says meekly, "I promise," in a monotone.

"I do not lie...much!" she adds as her conscience kicks in.

"You must leave now, before they track you down," she says in a serious tone. She swirls away from him, her skirt brilliant in the afternoon sunlight, like an exotic bird.

Swiftly, she leaps on her horse, seated like one leading a troupe to war, hair blowing against the wind. Her silk dress clings to her soft curved breasts, showing their promise and tantalisation of all red blooded men.

The exercise renders her cheeks with a warm glow, like a pink rose in bloom, Garty thinks. *A dark side lurks in this lovely rose, a black heart that worries me as much as her dramatic side woos my heart.*

She speaks from her mount as if she is some casual teacher giving straight forward directions to a pupil.

"Ride along the narrow way until you come to a crossing. Turn left and carry on for fifteen minutes. Work your way towards the bridge. Then you can see the inn in the distance. Not many folk know this route, but be careful, highwaymen live around here!" She looks at him and then away into the distance, assessing her own route while he considers her words.

"Thank you kindly," he says meaningfully. He waves goodbye, but she has already vanished into the woods, hidden by foliage. "Farewell," he shouts in vain.

Garty rides towards the inn, concocting plans to continue his commission. Surely he shall meet with her again? His heart is divided, sore and bleeding with wildest thoughts of beautiful females on horseback. *My dreams should fade in time,* he thinks miserably?

In the meantime, Axemanix's hit men have reached the Gypsies' camp and they are busily trying to locate a member of the tribe in order to uncover information. They bang noisily on Janda's door, "Let us in. We wish to speak with you," says a voice that sounds like a saw moving on hardwood.

Janda the clairvoyant opens her small door and stares into the faces before her. As her view widens she sees three men of mighty appearance, big, strong, with leather and velvet garments trimmed with pure gold. Animal furs drape over their shoulders with tiny frozen faces on one end that look like dead foxes or even dead red bears!

The face that leads the way is one with keen clear eyes, black as night. His face is bony, yet flushed with the faintest tint of pink. His nose spreads to fill in a lot of space between the rest of his face. It appears as if someone has boxed him hard. His lips are narrow and his hair darkest red, as fire. Gypsy Janda did not feel afraid of these men, for she had encountered such folk for most of her fifty years. Her fear had long dissipated with life's rough and tumble.

"Ye cannot pass this door lest you cross my palm with silver," she says, determinedly. Her eyes pierce into his thoughts.

The man steps away in shock. Who was this woman who defied a man who could possibly be the king's advisor in a few months when Axemanix came to the throne?

Gypsy Janda had covered her head and face with a black lace veil, which she used cleverly to disguise herself and mystify others.

The man stares at her for a moment, contemplating whether to push her or give her a coin. A man with ebony hair standing beside him on a lower step of the van entrance hands him a silver coin.

"Here, give it to her," he suggests.

Their leader takes the coin and placed it in the woman's palm.

She heaves a sigh, shoves the coin somewhere in a pocket and invites the three men inside.

"You may come in and sit down," she orders. "But wipe your filthy boots on that mat there," she commands. They obey without hesitation!

The three men fill the van space almost to capacity, with their animal skin clothing, including clutter of animal skins and game furs all over their necks, arms and around their waists. Signs of their previous spoils and class distinction!

On the very same table where she had spoken to Garty minutes before, there is now a magnificent crystal ball on a stand of topaz and crystal. It looks impressive to her visitors. She notices that they stare at the round ball with wonderment. Next to the ball, she lays three packs of cards, black, red and yellow. They lay face down on the table that she and Garty had shared a golden drink of pure apple juice.

"You," she points a long bony finger with very long nails painted black, at the first man.

"I shall tell thee what thy fortune will be," she says, using her mysterious voice that immediately mesmerises her victims.

The man sits down, bumping the table and almost ended up on the floor. He morphs into shock. All his life he had desired to visit a gypsy fortune teller, but had never done so. He waits, his eyes and mouth wide open. The other two men stood behind him, hypnotised.

The woman peers into the crystal ball and utters words in a strange language. Her hands wave over the globe as the men watch in fascination. She bangs her hands on the table.

"What did you see?" The man asks, his face turned ghostly white.

She shakes her head and stares into his eyes. "I cannot say what I saw because it is..." she pauses.

"Pick a card," she commands him as she picks a pack of cards and fans it out towards him. His shaking hand moves closer and he picks a card, passes it to her. With slow movements and deep thought, she places the card on the table before him. It has the figure of a Jack with a scythe in his hand.

"Pick another one," she commands. He does so and she places that one right side up next to the first. The picture is that of a King wearing a crown of gold.

"Another," she says, holding the pack towards him. He chose another and she places that card right side up next to the other two. It is a picture of a Queen.

She looks up slowly into the man's face. "Do not speak of these things outside of these walls," she warns. The man shook his head so much she could feel the flies and spiders rushing away. She had him under her power now. She rose up. "That is all," she says.

The man with the dead animals on his shoulders jumped up awkwardly, "What are you saying? You told me nothing," he says.

Chapter 12

"Cross my palm with silver," Janda says in a monotone voice. The second man, who carried the purse gave him a silver coin. It is larger than the first one they gave her.

Her eyes light up somewhat, and behind the veil, she make a happy gurgling sound.

"That is better! Now I shall tell thee things I should not know of thee, for I know thee not." She pauses and the man waits with his mouth open.

"Your name is Scythe Man, and you come from another place, another time." She pauses. The man she calls "Scythe" is shocked. His knees begin to shake.

"You come on a quest for a royal and you shall continue this quest on behalf of the royal. But there is a road that you should not travel, for upon it you will find danger lurking. A woman will wail when you do not return."

She stands upright.

"That is enough. I am tired," she says, leaning with both arms on the table, head bent. The three men stare at her for a moment.

"That is a load of rubbish," says the third man, who spoke for the first time. He is young, barely in his twenties, with fair hair and a ruddy countenance. He wears the finest black velvet cape with gold clasps on the shoulders and across his well hewn chest.

The first man, the one with the dead animals in his furry cape says, "No, she is right. I am Scythe, nobody knows that! I came from another land that I did not disclose... Everything she said is as true as the day we are here."

"Surely she knew of you before, somewhere?" The dark haired man suggested as tensions flare.

Scythe raises his hand. He slams a dagger in her fine table. Janda's face lifts and her eyes are daggers. He rises up tall before the woman. His head, adorned with a black velvet hat trimmed with gold appear awesome to the woman.

She looks up into his bird type eyes and moves her lips. Her voice is a metronome sing-song tone of voice.

"Would ye kill me then? For telling truth?" She asks. "And ruin my valuable table? Once loved by my great grandmother..., who haunts her enemies now!"

He snatches his knife and holds it aloft for a few moments as if his hand is stuck in mid air, ready to strike her head. Janda's eyes stare into Scythe's face, disempowering him. His eyes flicker and he returns to reality as the knife comes down with his attitude. He shoves it into his pouch on his hip.

"Hah! If we stay here all day listening to this gobble de gook, we will never catch our prey. And I am not talking about rabbits either," he says through clenched teeth. He throws back his head and laughs. The woman waits for a few moments of paradoxical ambience, overwhelming merriment and deepest gloom mingling within her caravan. She has had enough! If they stay much longer, she will surely die a horrible death, or shall kill them all with her sword and pistol, hidden, yet within her grasp! She shakes her head. They are not worth her energy. Slowly, her voice becomes loud and commanding again.

"I have given my secrets to you. Now, be on your way." Her index finger is pointed upwards and her lips grimly set. She speaks with such force that the men hurry out of her caravan, almost tripping over each others' feet in the rush to get out. Fear moves them on their way to catch the prey they are assigned to. The man she named 'Scythe' in her head, is the last to leave. He turns towards the woman, his eyes fill with admiration.

"I shall return," he says, smiling. Suddenly she feels a warmth towards this man. He believes her truth and she respects that.

"I shall look forward to meeting with ye again, alone is best," she adds carefully, so that the other two cannot hear their words.

He shakes her hand, imprinting her palm with a solid golden coin he has reserved for this day. "For repairs to thy table."

They depart with some noise. Other members of the Gypsy family stay hidden for fear of being run through, or worst still, being taken away and tortured.

The woman decides it is time for a nice cup of floral tea and she begins to sing in her strangely beautiful, eerie voice as she hides her coins underneath the carpet near her feet, in a secret little box beyond the wooden floor.

"I sing ye a song of travellers who wander across the globe, finding love and passion in places they were told…"

She closes her eyes for a moment of peace!

****

Garty waits in the woods for a time, to ensure Crystalina is not riding this way. On the way out through the thicket that suddenly opened out to a clearing, he notices an old building. At first he assumes it to be a ruin, but riding closer, he inspects a sign that is broken on one chain, fallen on its side. He twists his head to read the words: GRACEFUL ORPHANAGE FOR CHILDREN. It is now worn and damaged, but he identifies the words after a few efforts. His heart beats soundly.

If the gypsy is correct, this is the place where the child was abandoned!

He stares at the facade of the building, large brown double doors, windows with square panes of glass, some filled with cardboard or other materials. The garden is overgrown, roses mixed with blackberry bushes, making everything look tangled and impossible to sort. He is about to turn away when he notices something moving inside a window. *It is definitely not a ghost*, he assures himself. *Well, better find out whether or not there are records of children here?*

This now seemed like a golden opportunity to fulfil his mission.

He pushes open a creaking gate that is covered in rust and barely standing in its hinges. Three steps, well-worn, dirty and chipped in places are its entrance. He steps up the three and stands in the rather large stone platform outside the front door, with its filthy little windows at the sides and its oxidised brass latch. He notices a rusted iron bell in a casing on the wall. He tugs the little string and feels dust and grime on his fingers. He wipes his hand on his thigh. *Would someone come out to talk to a stranger,* he wonders? Just as he feels like giving up hope, he hears the door click and creak. He views a nose and eyes and then bushy hair and a narrow chin peering at him. Long fingers hold the door close to its edge, as if they needed something to hold onto. *Fear surely moves this person,* Garty thinks, moving back a step so as to give them a chance to see his person. He has no gun visible on him.

"What do you want?" A female voice speaks.

"Good day Madam, Garty says. Sorry to trouble you, but I am on the King's business and I was wondering if you may be able to assist."

"We have no food. Go away," she says, attempting to close the door. Garty shoved his booted toe in the gap and said, "I am so sorry, but I do not need food. I need information about a child who lived here."

The door slowly opened a little more, so that he sees the whole frame of the person. The woman is in her fifties or sixties, maybe older even, and she is wearing a type of uniform suited to her station, navy cotton dress under a white apron that is drab and faded, with several patches and a number of badly repaired rips and holes. Her dress was ink coloured in its hey day, now faded and topped by a tarnished yellowish collar.

"Are you its parent or guardian?" She asks. She stamps her feet as she speaks, as if ordering children to go backwards away from some adult conversation.

So, there were children here and not too long ago I figure, Garty reasons, picking up her thought patterns. *Maybe some children live here even now? She is hiding something!*

"I am neither parent nor guardian, but am searching for a lost female child. Commissioned by King Justice Swanfeather of Kallai."

Her demeanour changes instantly. She presses her hand to her sternum and utters a cry.

"I come from Kallai Central, born on the First Day of December..." she says. "Mrs Irma Nagg," at your service. "Please come in! I thought you were a stranger!" Suddenly friendly, she beckons to him.

Relieved, Garty steps into the wide hallway with black and white tiled floor akin to a checker board. A wide stairway leads up to rooms above.

On either side of the stairway are rooms, dark and dismal and badly in need of maintenance. His heart lurches for its needs. *I cannot fix the whole world,* he decides thus commanding his rational to earth and reality here today.

"Come into our dining room," she says, leading the way into a room nearby.

He notices that *her shoes are worn and her black stockings show a number of small holes. How terrible for this woman, to be so poverty stricken*, he thinks? *Where is her husband?* His thoughts subside as they enter the room.

"Please, be seated, Sir," she says, indicating the collapsed armchair near a circular table, polished and stained with many stains. A vase stands in the centre with flowers as faded as the walls. He smells rancid aromas emitting from the vase, but he choses not to mention the fact. He does not wish to intimidate this lady at any cost.

She sits in a wooden chair that creaks as she moves slightly. Her hands fold in her lap and her ankles cross as she waits like a school girl waits for a headmaster to administer his orders. A deep pity crawls over Garty as he struggles with his posture in the collapsed armchair. He tries to sit straight up and act politely. After all, he is a perfect gentleman, so must suffer discomfort at times. He binds his fingers together and leans forward, taking a moment to stare at the floor before lifting his head and opening his mouth. *How shall I begin?* She is staring into his eyes, piercing his soul. He begins his interrogation.

"There was a certain female babe brought here to the orphanage nineteen or twenty years ago. I am trying to find her!"

He stares at the woman's expression that changes and relaxes into an almost comical mode.

Her mouth reminds me of an egg in its oval shape, with a thin border around it.

"Sir," she says, as if answering for something she had not done and had been blamed for, "we have had hundreds of girls and boys left on our doorstep over the years. Twenty years ago there were many poor mothers." She stops for a moment's breath and Garty speaks.

"This one was special. She was wrapped in scarlet," he says, grasping the edges of his cape for emphasis. The woman stares straight ahead, but she is obviously trying to remember something.

"I was head governess here at that time."

At least she remembers something that happened now almost twenty years ago! This may be a breakthrough, thinks Garty, leaning closer, but not too close. His back ached in this position.

"Do you have records for that year?"

The woman is quiet for a while.

"We have been operating for over one hundred years you know? Until we closed our doors a couple of years ago, due to lack of finance," she adds in a heavy tone. "Very disappointing for the little ones with nowhere to go," she says, heaving a huge sigh. "I do have records in our filing system, if you would like to see those," she adds unexpectedly.

What a brainwave! Garty thinks. *It is the very thought I am meditating upon. Can she have sensed my thoughts and stolen them? This is hopeful. Actual records would be invaluable.*

"I certainly would appreciate that," Garty says, suddenly stirred. Hope flickers once again for his mission.

"Come with me."

Chapter 13

Mrs Nagg limps her way down the hall and into a small room filled almost to head height in square, oak brown drawers with brass handles. A little ticket with alphabetical indication was on most of the drawers.

"These are somewhat shabby, but all records are in these files," she says. "Do you know the name of the child?"

Garty is confounded instantly. He has no idea what her name was when the Gypsies brought her here, or if she had a name at all?

"She didn't have a name, just baby!" he says reluctantly, thinking, *well, that is certainly the end of that investigation. She will banish me from here now! I must sound uninformed.*

The woman surprises him once again.

"Then she will be in here!" Carefully, she pulls out a drawer near the ground. "Many of our children had no names at all, and we gave them names." She pulls open the file that is quite stuck together over years of moisture, dust and neglect. Garty reaches over to help her but she shooed him away. "Go away. Leave it to me."

There are numerous files in a row. He watches as Mrs Nagg rummages through dusty brown files that crumble at her touch. She takes out a bundle as if she has won a prize. She places them on the round table.

"These all have no names at all! Your best chance!" Her job is now done as far as she is concerned.

"May I take a look at what is inside?" Garty asks.

"You most certainly can do so. I must go and water the chickens, otherwise we will have no breakfast. "I do love a boiled egg, don't you?" She didn't wait for his reply. "I shall leave you here, if you don't mind, for a time," she suggests. Her face has brightened and her mission is clear, to help friends and he was now her friend.

"I shall take good care of them, friend. I do enjoy a boiled egg very much!"

She threw back a grin as he said that. He pleased her very much it seemed.

Garty stared at the pile of dust-impregnated brown files. He despaired at the thought of trying to figure out what mattered and what did not, in the pile of files scattered on the table, *but every little clue helps*, he surmises, as he has learned over almost five years. He thumbs through one by one. He reads the scribbled headings: gender of child; state of child; date and time; comments. He soon finds a speedy method of working. Garty has learned how to quickly discern what is valuable information and what is not. He separates the ones with earlier or later dates, gender of males from females. That brings the pile of around 100 down to 50 or so. That is more doable, he reasons. He reads all the little comments looking for one word: SCARLET.

His finger races over the words like flint or even as fast as lightning. His eyes race with his finger, keeping up the pace, reminding him of his glorious race with Crystalina today! *What a joy,* he muses, smiling to himself, and at once loses track of his project. He pauses for one moment, closing his eyes and believing he was hugging her, caressing her tiny perfectly round breasts, indulging his manly senses. A bird squawks.

Opening his eyes, he scolds his soul for its departure from its business. *Get on with it, man!* Beginning once again, he harnesses his mind. After some time, he has checked almost thirty of the fifty files and still not seen the word he wanted or something of note.

He remembered that Crystalina said her mother, a true Gypsy, was also a liar. He did not wish to believe it as he felt that she told him the truth, and she did not ask him for money, a very honourable trait for someone from a people group with such a bad reputation in this area. As his finger moves to the last ten records, he stops thumbing. The word scarlet is written thereupon, in red ink. His eyes boggle for a moment. He has to read the whole report, which is filled with notes and markings. Could he take a page from a gypsy's book and remove this file? He dared not wait for Mrs Nagg to turn up and give him a lecture and take the files away. He needed more time! It was getting late and he felt very hungry. He could not stay for dinner because he knew there was no dinner cooking here. Thoughts of

Mrs Bouchée's fine roasts, pies, stews, grills and baked goods arouse his hunger pains loudly.

I have to do this! He takes the folder with the notes and slips them inside his cape with its many pockets hidden from the naked eye. Just then Mrs Nagg stands in the doorway. Garty's eyes leap in surprise. *Did she see him taking the file?*

"Did you find what you wanted?" she asks.

He stands up. "I may have. I just need to check a few more details," he adds as he feels the stolen stiff paper in his side searing his conscience. "I must away for I have another engagement to attend." He stands up and stares into her face. He must get this file out of here pronto and get his own rear end out as well.

I can bear this place no longer!

"I shall keep you informed about the king's business. And hopefully, we shall meet again one day in Kallai Central where you were born on the first day of December? Firstly, I must put these files back into their places…"

"Do not bother yourself about that. I shall take care of these," she says. "The chickens are watered and I found two eggs," she says with a grin.

"How nice for you," Garty says, returning her smile.

"I am glad I could help a friend," she says. "Please return whenever you wish to check those details you mentioned."

She is already picking up some of the scattered pieces of paper and shuffling them into a neat pile, like a pack of very large playing cards. Garty watches with his heart in his mouth. He can barely breathe wondering if she may miss one piece of her valuable files. But, she seems happy with his interest and smiles during the process of saying goodbye.

"I shall see thee away," says Mrs Nagg, standing straight up and hobbling to the front door. "The latch is a trifle sticky," she says, tugging at the brass knob. "Come back and I shall boil thee an egg."

"Thank you kindly." *Let me out of here!*

The last thing he remembers about her is the long bony hand holding the door ajar and her eye glued upon his person.

Brill had helped himself to a nice snack of wild grasses and flowers nearby, along with a clear pond that held darting goldfish. The pond is totally empty now, and Brill is happy. He hoped they are hidden behind foliage or underneath some small rocks. However, he has his doubts and feels that Brill may have had a snack of fish. Garty does not admonish Brill but pats his neck. *A horse is a horse and can do as it pleases.*

"Thanks for waiting for me, friend," he says. The horse throws his head up and neighs with satisfaction.

"Okay, we are going home now," he says, leaping on his back, settling down and with his fingers on the tip of his pistol, retrieved from beneath his saddle, kicks his knees gently into Brill's sides, sparking a fine trot along the now darkening laneway as the sun creeps slowly behind the hills finished with its long day.

"It has been such a long day, Brill. I am famished!"

I still could not stomach Mrs Nagg's boiled egg. I lied.

Garty rode his faithful horse a little more slowly, to ensure the horse is kept in good stead. *This faithful horse has endured this day just as well as me,* he reckons.

Dusk has almost blanketed the streets of Scatt as Garty rides quietly into its sombre hub. A few dim street lamps are lit.

Pulling on the reins, "Whoa boy," he says, scanning the streets in the dim lighting. Lamps cast shadows over the inn's facade and its perimeters. Garty cannot fail to notice a small sulky and three unfamiliar horses tied at the Maud Inn. Brill snorts in excitement.

Steering Brill towards a back street, Garty pulls his hat a little closer to his eyes over his forehead and holds firmly to the grip of his pistol. He senses instantly who these folk might be and his heart beats at double its usual pace.

"Quietly," he whispers to Brill, who has a knack of being able to move without a sound no matter how rocky or hard the earth below its hoofs. His steed understands his command and walks quietly, barely making a clink. Silently Garty dismounts at the back of the inn, where everything is quieter. Lamps are glowing along the passageway and a few servants can be seen darting in and out of buildings, which is their normal procedure at evening when food is required by guests or casual visitors alike.

He leads Brill into his allocated stable and almost scares the pants off young Bubba, who is raking the hay.

"Sorry Sir," she says, pausing her work, looking into Garty's face with an expression that appears as if she has seen a ghost!

"No, no, please do not apologise. I should be sorry for frightening you," says Garty, speaking quietly. "Thank you for taking care of Brill for me."

Bubba bows slightly and he notices a small hint of a smile on her face.

"I see you have guests tonight?" he adds in a familiar tone.

"Yes, we do," she says, nodding her head. "I have new friends to take care of, my favourite kind of friends," she adds, obviously happy to enjoy animal interaction, indicating the stables alongside, where there are two more steeds enjoying a nose bag. "We don't have any more room for the other pair, but I shall work something out," she says with a glint in her eyes.

He loves seeing her so happy creating comfortable places for horses.

She was definitely created for this job, he muses.

"Do you have any idea where they have come from?" Garty asks, pushing his luck to find out a bit more about these guests.

She shakes her head.

Chapter 14

"All I know is that they arrived about an hour ago and they had a sweat up," Bubba says.

"I had to cool them down with a wash and brush to help bring their temperatures and breathing level again. But it was okay then," she says.

"They are happy now!"

A figure appears from around the corner. "What are you doing here, there is work to do, you know?" said Ted, her associate and superior at times.

"Sorry Sir, I will just give Brill his nose bag," said Bubba, obviously shaking and worried.

Ted had not seen Garty waiting in the shadows.

Good evening Ted, I see that you are busy. I do apologise for taking Bubba's time. I am going to my room now," he says.

"Sir, I didn't see you there! It is just that we have more guests tonight and we have a lot to do."

"I understand," Garty says.

Ted rushes off, carrying a silver tray with drinks thereon into one of the cabins at the back of the building. Garty follows his trail until he moves into the shadows. Being dusk, with darkness descending, it is difficult to see clearly. Two lamps emit a glow in the dark.

"Musdo!" Garty hears a familiar voice as he heads to his quarters, through a small walkway.

"Good evening Mrs Bouchée," says Garty, tipping his hat. *This is a surprise,* he thinks. *Usually she is inside rather than out at this time of day. What is going on?*

"Be quiet," is her only answer. She keeps herself hidden near the apple trees.

Something is clearly amiss, Garty figures.

He moves closer.

She looks around before she speaks and fear is emanating from her eyes. He pays attention to her words.

"You must get out of here as quickly as possible. These men are asking about you, what you are doing here and how much money you are paying people for information? They pretended they had information, but they do not! They have arms!" Her hands grip his shoulders and he feels them shaking in fear.

"They want to search your room! I persuaded them to eat and drink first after their long journey. You have very little time to get away. However, I have done my best and given them free run of my very best Mature Apple Wine," she says with a twinkle in her eye as she steps near the lamp.

Garty is shocked to hear these words.

Hw was keen to look through information he had found and enjoy a relaxing bath. He was also very hungry. But, he is more keen to stay alive!

"Listen, Mrs. Bouchée, thank you for telling me these things. Somebody must have told them I am staying here."

He scoops a handful of gold coins from his velvet pouch and presses them into her sweaty palm.

"There is no need. You are a King's ambassador."

She holds the gold coins and takes a deep breath. "Nevertheless, kindness is a marvellous trait, so, thank you!"

She places her hand in her pocket and the golden coins are out of sight.

"Go on quickly," she says. "Here is something to take with you" she adds, handing him a home made linen bag that held some freshly baked bread.

Garty was wondering where the homey smell came from. Fresh bread! This is a big risk she is taking, he knows, and frowns for an instant as worry sweeps over his heart.

"This will see you through. Now, there is a fine inn that is not too far away from here. Turn left at the junction and travel for about five miles. Turn left again and you will see a fine old inn. It is owned by my sister Etty, who will care for you. Not many folk stay there for it is rather small and cosy, but you will be comfortable in a feather bed. Etty's Inn, it is called."

Garty's head is spinning with so many urgencies happening at once. He runs his hand across his forehead.

"Thank you," he says.

"I must go," Mrs Bouchée says, looking around and moving silently through the trees towards the kitchen.

"May God go with thee...!" Garty says softly. Mrs Bouchée's life could be in danger! Then Garty notices Ted watching from the lower sheds where the chickens are kept. He looks away as Garty catches his eyes. He beckons Ted who reluctantly comes towards him. *After all,* Garty thinks, *I am still their guest here!*

"Can you please help Bubba with my horse? I shall be departing shortly," he asks Ted.

"Yes, Sir! I thought you were staying the whole week? And where might you be heading off to?" He asks.

Garty immediately wonders, *would he ask me such a private question? This is not a Servant's right!* His answer was measured.

"On the King's business, as usual," he replies a little curtly.

Ted reacts by shuffling away a few steps, stops and mumbles and apology.

"Sorry Sir! Didn't mean to be inquisitive, just caring about you, Sir, and your horse!" Ted mumbles his explanation. He looks exceedingly embarrassed.

"Thank you," Garty replies through his teeth. "Your concern is appreciated and not warranted!" He does not disclose any more information.

Garty walks to his quarters to pack and leave as speedily as possible.

Concentrating on his job in hand, Garty places the cloth with warm bread aside and pulls out every drawer to ensure that nothing personal remains behind. Gathering his toiletries, including his boot polish and brush, he remembers that he is still wearing the hand made boots from the cobbler.

"Shucks," he moans. He shakes his head in his own disappointment. It was not like him to forget anything, but this time, he had forgotten all about the boots.

Drat, I forgot and now these fit more snugly, he muses. *It looks like I must return to this town and retrieve my old boots.*

He is also listening to the sounds around him as he gathers his stuff. He hears merry laughter in the dining room of the Maud Inn and sighs.

Mrs Bouchée's fine wine is doing its job, he reflects, remembering her quiet conversation with him. *Now I must take a chance to get away from these highway robbers before being taken captive or even worse, murdered!*

His blood runs cold as he reminds himself for whom these highwaymen might be working on behalf of, and what could happen to him if he was captured?

He has so many notes and information about folk in these parts that their lives might be put into danger too! He almost wished that he had destroyed all the bits of paper, trinkets and notes. He decides to do so as soon as practicable.

I must find a way to dispose of these personal notes for safety sake. I have left everything too late!

His ledger is full of people's names and private details. He hopes that this leg of his mission will not end in a radical disaster after so many years doing hard work and due diligence! *There is no time now!*

He moves steadily and quietly towards the stables where Brill is still nibbling on a nice bag of apples. Bubba is stroking his neck, watched by Ted, who is now sweeping the stalls. He looks up with fear into Garty's face as he steps into the stable yard.

"Thank you for caring for Brill, Ted," Garty says, throwing a silver coin towards Ted. Ted catches it flying as if it was a cricket ball and presses it hurriedly into his top pocket. He smiles happily. He is showing his big teeth in all their glory. Garty then slips Bubba two silver coins! She plummets them smoothly into the back pocket of her livery pants. She nods her thanks with her eyes. Quietly, her hand moves Brill from the feeding trough and he obeys eagerly. *She has a touch of an angel with a great beast,* he muses.

Garty places his saddle bag over the hollow of his horses' back and instantly glides into the rider's seat. He feels for his pistol butt and breathes deeply, flinging his scarlet cape behind his shoulders. The horse prances a little for a moment, sensing the urgency.

Riding his horse as silently as possible, Garty heads through the back gate, surprising the chickens who squawk as he passes by.

Garty glances behind but the hunters are nowhere to be seen. Feeling rather nervous he knows these fellows are rotten eggs.

Devotees of Axemanix no doubt, and not good in any way, small or great. I must avoid them at all costs, or everything will be lost, even my life.

He rides along narrow tracks off the main highways, spending time being smacked by overhanging branches of large sycamore trees and dozens of wild animals screeching from their homes, especially bats that fly a little too close for comfort with their colony of family members flocking and screeching nearby as night falls deeper and darker before his horses' hoofs.

He rides for some time and fatigue begins to cloud his mind. *Where is Etty's Inn?* Even as his hope wanes, to his surprise and ultimate delight, he spies a building with a large chimney smoking valiantly into the night sky. Instinctively, Garty knows this is the place, away from every other living creature in the world, it seems.

How clever was Mrs Bouchée, he thinks, *hoping beyond hope that this is indeed the inn of her sister, Etty!*

He can barely believe it was a mere five miles from the Maud Inn! But, perhaps he has travelled a little more distance by avoiding the main highway. And he certainly had avoided highway men robbing him.

Just having my purse replenished is a blessing. Now Garty fears that fact may be a curse because he carries quite a lot of gold and silver, the desire of highway robbers.

I shall refuse to meditate on that fact!

Chapter 15

Garty stops and takes in the view before him as usual before proceeding into possible danger.

The building appears smaller than the Maud, obviously a farm house remodelled into an inn. A small sign at the front gate, along with a dim lamp, indicates its nature. *Its front is open and gracious, inviting in the daylight*, he decides. Now, *it is dark and even dangerous* as the horse treads lightly on soft grass. The door looms dark with its jambs displaying dim side lights of lead glass allowing a shimmer of light to emit. Sliding silently from his mount, he sums up the matter. A large brass bell catches a glow. He tugs the bell and waits, speaking softly to Brill, who seems keen to trim the grass down a smidgen with his mighty teeth.

"Stop, Brill," he whispers. The horse neighs lightly, but stops and waits with his master.

A flustered man, with a rosy complexion and a night cap opens the door slightly.

"Who be ye? He asks in a loud voice.

"Maud Bouchée sent me hither," Garty replies.

"Friend or foe?" The man asks as if there was some war going on and a person must take sides.

"Friend, surely a friend," Garty says, almost begging to be allowed in. *Please let me in!*

The man opens the door and his hand is extended. He holds a lit candle.

"Come in friend," he says. "Wipe thy feet."

"First, my horse must bed down," Garty says. "And be fed."

"I be there in a tick of a grandfather clock," the Inn Keeper says.

Closing the door in Garty's face, he disappears. Garty waits, becoming a little uneasy. Fifteen minutes later, the man, clothed in oilskin cape and boots, holding an oil lamp, bustles through the door.

"Follow me," he says, hobbling as he walks along the pathway and towards some old sheds. His oil lamp creaks, his boots squeak and even his oilcloth cape squeaks. Garty has no problem following him.

"Here is where the animals sleep," he holds the oil lamp up so that Garty can take a good view of its suitability.

"We do have horse feed in this barrel, he says, pointing to a rather large round barrel in the corner. It is filled with hay and oats.

"That looks sufficient," Garty says. "And water?" He asks.

"Over here," the man redirected Garty to a long trough nearby. It has a pump standing above it.

"You can pump more water if you want to" he says.

Garty is satisfied.

"Is there a stable hand?" Garty asks.

The man shakes his head. "I am the gopher here. I can take your horse and give him a warm blanket for the night?"

"Thank you. That is kind of you," Garty says, unsaddling his mount and loading his person with knapsack and saddle bag, saddle, along with his rifle and pistol.

"Sack is my name" the man said, holding his free hand to Garty. "Sorry, I will take some of those things," says Sack.

Garty gives him his saddle to hold, while they shake hands.

"Garty Musdo," Garty says. "I appreciate your kindness."

"Not at all," said Sack, who begins a search for the blanket he promised. "I left it here somewhere," he mumbles, tripping over something in the dim light.

"Where can I leave these?" Garty asks, holding on to his whip and straps, along with other items.

"Drop your tack there," the man points to a shelf on the far side.

Garty heads over there and releases some of his load, turning back towards Sack. He keeps his saddle bag over his shoulder.

"Go on inside Garty, for Etty knows you are coming and is preparing supper."

Garty's stomach is grumbling badly now, and he longs for a nice hot meal. He had taken the bread that Mrs Bouchée had given him when it was hot. It is cold now. But, he thought he might get to eat it later if the meal proved insufficient.

"Here, take this!" Sack says, addressing Garty, handing him the oil lamp.

"Thank you, Sack. What will you do without it?"

"I can do all I need to blindfolded." Sack laughs as he says this. It is a dark night and the moon is barely visible, only in snatches of light as the clouds part for a moment or two.

"You go on in now! Use the back door, it's open. I shall follow thee later," says the man, busily covering the horse in a warm woollen blanket. Brill seems satisfied as he nibbles at the food in the barrel.

Garty finds the back door of the establishment and sure as Sack had said, the door opens as he pushes on the handle. It creaks a little. There is a dim light in an entrance and he sees doors on either side with numbers on them.

He made his way through the short corridor and into a dining area. There is a table with a couple dining, a young woman with golden hair and pale face. The man with her is thin, bony and probably taller than Garty, who is six feet tall. He cannot ascertain this until the man stands. They glance his way as he enters the room. The aroma of cooking fills his nostrils.

A woman comes hurriedly from a nearby kitchen, leaving sizzling noises in her wake. She wipes her hands on her apron and seems unduly flustered.

"Good evening, Sir, did you need to eat now?" She asks.

He sighs inwardly and says, "It is a late hour, but I should appreciate a hot meal. If that is not too much trouble for thee, Madam?"

"No indeed! We were about to close the kitchen when you rang the door bell, however, that not a problem. I see you are overburdened with luggage. Would you like to put your things in your room or keep them with you?"

Garty quickly sums her up. She appears younger than Mrs Bouchée and quite similar in appearance, robust, with keen eyes and flushed cheeks, beneath her grey baker's cap, her mousey hair is tucked in. Her apparel is a little less fashionable than Maud's, even dowdy, with charcoal being her gown colour, causing her countenance to appear wan. *She is also a little more flustered in demeanour,* he deems.

She ducks into the office in the front entrance and has a key in her hand when she returns a few moments later.

"Come now, put those things in a safe place and then you can enjoy a bite to eat. I know how hungry men can be!"

"Thank you." Garty follows her to a room nearby. She opens the door. He looks inside and is quite surprised at its generous size. There is a four poster bed, plenty of cupboards, a lamp and a small table with drawers.

"Perfect," he exclaims.

She seems pleased with his response. She leaves him to prepare his supper.

He hopes it tastes as good as Mrs. Bouchée's food, but has doubts! Inn's rarely produced such homey and delicious foods comparable to Maud Bouchée's establishment.

He finds a mirror on the wall above a water jug and basin and washes his face, drying it with a fluffy towel on a hook. He tidies his tossed hair. He removed his cape and sits on the side of the bed with his head in his hands for a few moments recovery. *Surely I am safe for now?*

"Good evening," Garty says as he passes by the young couple dining in the dining room.

They reply politely, "Good evening," and continue eating and drinking.

Garty sits down at a table nearby. A few moments later, Etty comes hurrying towards him, carrying a tray with a dish of sorts.

She smiles as she places the meal before Garty.

I might eat a horse right now. Not a horse exactly, he corrects his thoughts. He would never eat Brill, his wonderful companion and ride for so many years now. He looks at the dish before him, reheated stew with a pile of what looks like rough potato mash on the side of the large porcelain plate. He could see a little steam, which cheered him up. *A hot meal!*

"Thank you. It looks hearty!" Garty says.

Etty is happy with that comment, and clears a few items away, including extra cutlery and glasses.

"Would you like something to drink?"

Garty orders apple juice, as he had become almost addicted to Mrs. Bouchée's delicious apple juices that seemed to lift his spirits remarkably well.

Garty starts to taste the food before him. It was not exactly delicious, *but it will fill a large gap in my growling stomach,* he reckons. It tastes a trifle cold in spots but he eats as much as he possibly can without choking. In the meantime, the couple quietly exit the dining room, leaving Garty alone with a number of oil lamps and a few candles strewn around the tables. He counts four tables and eight candles.

"Thank you, I have had sufficient, and appreciated," he says to Etty as she appears from the shadows to remove his empty plate.

Very civil, he notes. *I trust Sack is still taking care of Brill, as he has not returned. Nevertheless, I trust the Innkeeper to care for Brill. Now I must be off to bed and rest. Another day awaits me tomorrow.* He heads for his room.

Garty falls into a deep sleep until sunrise. He barely hears the knock on his door. Madam Etty hurries in with a nice hot cup of tea.

"I trust this will cheer you up," she says. "For 'tis a wonderful day with the birds singing and the sun shining brightly! I took the liberty of adding sugar and cream," Etty says with a twinkle in her eyes.

She knows what men like, for sure, Garty thinks.

"Thank you very much," Garty says, as he takes the porcelain cup and saucer from her hands. He is a little distracted being in his night shirt and long johns undergarment, but she didn't seem to notice or care about his appearance. She pulls apart the curtains to bring light into the darkness. Garty flinches at the blast of light for a moment as it pours into the darkened room.

"Breakfast will be ready in thirty minutes," she adds as her large figure disappears from his view and the door shuts behind her.

Before enjoying a leisurely breakfast Garty determines to visit Brill to see how he fared through the night in a strange location. After a quick toilette, abandoning the empty cup and saucer on the small table in his room, he heads out to the stables. As he walks through the property, he sums up his quarters. He feels quietly pleased that its location avails his viewing the local roadways. He will remain alert for any highway men coming to visit him for unknown reasons. He pats Brill and holds out a handful of feed on his palm.

"Good boy," he says. The horse is not the only one there. Next door to Brill he notices a couple of horses, and he sees another stable further along the way. There is also a sulky parked in the yard, *possibly belonging to the young couple I met last night.*

Leaving Brill with a good drink of water nearby, he heads for the dining area once again. Its ambience is more akin to a formal dining area this morning. At night it had seemed mystique and romantic with all the candles burning. Now there are no lamps burning and the sun brings with it the natural lighting, giving the room a soft coziness.

He notices the young woman is seated at the same table she shared with the man on the previous evening. He sits at the table adjacent, in case they may enjoy a short conversation. He is, of course, always investigating possibilities of his quest for a princess. *Every young woman is a possibility*, he thinks.

"Good morning," the woman says, smiling his way. She is reading the local 'Jael Newspaper', which she places on the table.

She appears friendly.

"Good morning," Garty bows slightly, rising to the occasion. Garty sits down again. "It's a fine day," he says conversationally. "Is your husband unwell?" He asks, *just in case there is a problem with the man she shared her dinner with in the evening before.*

She laughs lightly. He notices her golden hair in the morning light, set upon her head like a tower, with a few strands flowing around her ears. *She seems exceedingly sweet,* he thinks, taking a deep breath. She suddenly stands up and moves a few steps to Garty's table, grasping the newspaper.

"May I?" She asks.

He immediately jumps up and holds the chair away from the table to enable her to be seated.

"I shall only stay a moment. My brother is engaged in his toiletry," she explains. "He was still asleep, but will join me shortly," she says, anxiously looking towards the doorway.

"I understand," Garty says. *Yes, I understand that this woman and man are siblings. The man had the upper hand as the woman is practically fearful for some reason.*

"Is he also your chaperone?" Garty asks. *I have met many folk in the area who appointed male siblings to chaperone their daughters. I am not surprised at all to see this type of arrangement.*

Chapter 16

"Yes," she answers, fear leaping into her dark blue eyes. He takes notice of her features as she looks into his face momentarily.

She seems to feel obligated to tell me a few items of interest about herself. Maybe there is an underlying problem here?

"I am Joanna Weasley," she says, putting forward her gloved hand. He takes it graciously and bends his lips to kiss her fingers. She blushes intensely, and he notices.

"I have come into this region to gain suitable employment as a governess," she explains, though Garty has not asked her business.

"Garty Musdo! I trust you have found success?" He asks her, smiling into her eyes.

"Not yet, Garty," she explains. "However, my brother is negotiating matters with some of his acquaintances in this district," she adds.

"I wish him success on your behalf," he replies. Garty moves his hand to his sketch pad. He feels compelled to sketch all the folk he had met in Scatt but not had time to complete, whilst his memory is sharp.

"Good morning, Sir," the deep voice echoes through the door.

"It's my brother Jazzon," she says softly. She quickly returns to her own table. Jazzon comes towards them with an angry countenance.

"I see you two have become acquainted?" Jazzon states, sitting down beside his sister.

"That is true," Garty says. He rises and extends his hand to Jazzon. "Garty," he says.

Jazzon does not reply or extend his hand in any sort of friendship. He stares down at Garty with a face of contempt.

"Joanna, this is outrageous!" He turns and addressed his sister gruffly.

"I am on the king's business," Garty interrupts Jazzon's dialogue with his sister.

"I am enquiring of everyone I meet," he adds, hoping to calm the situation a little.

"I see. Well, in that case, I will accept an apology. For my sister is a single woman and she needs complete protection from pretenders."

"I do respect that and give you my apologies most profusely. May I buy you a drink, Sir?" Garty further extends his apologetic rhetoric.

"You may," Jazzon replies. "Rum!"

Garty places the order as soon as he notices Madam Etty.

Jazzon seemed a little happier after having consumed the glass of rum so early in the day, Garty muses. *It was worth it,* he thinks.

Later in the day, Garty sets up a little patch for himself in the garden at the back of the establishment where small green cast iron tables and chairs are situated. He sits with his portfolio, a rather large pile of bits of paper, his sketch pad and his charcoal pencil. His mind remains active for a while as he recalls the information from the inn at Scatt! He pondered the jewels taken from the crib and makes a sketch of what it may have looked like. His portrait of Queen Bianca is becoming smudged, bringing with it in difficulties in matching confit sketches. He had begun a new sketch of the queen, using the damaged portrait.

"That's a nice work of art," a voice startles him in his reverie. He looks up to see Miss Weasley standing nearby. He stands up, dropping his pencil on the ground.

"Sorry, I did not mean to startle you," she says , bending to pick up his tool before he can reach it. She hands it to him. "You are an artist?" she asks.

He feels heat sweeping over his face. "I am not an artist, not by trade, just sketching for information, profiler is more like my task here," he adds. *Her presence stirs this feeling of excitement that I cannot explain.*

"I think it looks lovely. You definitely have a talent." She pauses, thinking for a moment.

"Please sit down, join me," says Garty. "Unless your brother objects?" he says.

"He has gone to see a gentleman friend in the district and shall be absent all day." She looks away for a moment, contemplating her brother's departure and mission. The hills are dotted with sheep around here and the growth is spasmodic.

"This is a great little hideaway, I mean, safe haven!" she says.

"Thank you. I shall take the pleasure of joining you for a little time," she says, as Garty hurriedly lifts the heavy iron chair, and places it for her to be seated.

"Thank you."

She places her gloves on the table. He cannot help but notice her beautiful countenance. She is not the pretty type, rather more the dramatic, interesting type. Her eyes are almost sleepy in descriptive terms, and her bosom is ample. *She is wearing a lighter outfit than she wore at evening meals,* he notes. It is a shade of light blue, *like a Springtime sky at noon.*

"Would you like me to order a drink for you?" Garty asks, rising as he speaks. "I shall find Etty or Sack?"

"A cool drink please. It is warming here, summer is nigh," she says, smiling at him.

How daunting are her plump lips! They are kissable to infinity!

Of course, he dares not say anything so personal to someone of such beauty and grandeur.

"Certainly," says Garty, rushing off to find Etty. Garty has worked out the floor plan already and knows where they cook meals and generally spend their days, in a little nook near the kitchen called a pantry!

He wants to ask Joanne questions before her brother returns, so feels a little rushed, even finding the proprietors seems stressful here. He almost bumps into Sack as he rushes through the little corridor near the kitchen. He is carrying two jugs and almost spills them all over Garty, but manages to steady his load in time.

"I was just looking for you," Garty says. "Miss Joanne would like a cool drink," he adds, staring at the jugs of cold lemonade.

"Ha! I must have listened to your conversations. Here are drinks, if ye don't mind?" He gives Garty the two jugs of drink. Garty takes them, gladly.

"We will need two drinking vessels as well," he says to Sack, who is already humming a tune and heading towards the pantry or kitchen.

"Of course," he replies in nonchalant fashion.

"Here you are, two full jugs of lemonade, freshly made, I believe. I smell lemons all over me," Garty says humorously.

"You are a lemonade genius," Joanne says, staring into Garty's face.

She is funny!

Her hair glows like a halo of spun gold and he almost drops the enamel jugs promptly.

How my fingers might disappear into this golden halo!

As he places the jugs on the small wobbly table, Sack shuffles towards them holding two clear fragile glasses. He places them on the table.

"Will that be all?" He asks, moving away, expecting no more orders until lunchtime.

"What about something sweet?" Joanne asks. "I feel like something small and sweet," she adds, smiling her adorable smile. Sack shrugs his shoulders and waves his hand.

"I shall check with the good woman," he says.

Garty pours the cool lemonade and they feel refreshed immediately even by its pungent aroma, delicious sweet-bitter taste and sparkles up their noses.

"It's just right," says Joanne.

Garty nods. He likes being with this woman. *She makes me feel like a gentleman, and is a picture to gaze at, not that I should gaze for too long,* he reminds his inner soul. He does not wish to cause her embarrassment.

"Now you can draw a picture of me," she says, sitting back a little, staring into his face.

He is totally smitten. He takes the charcoal in his trembling fingers.

"Whatever the lady wants, the lady gets?" Garty's glib reply is tinged with his joy. He is a trifle shocked at his own response. He has not been involved too much with ladies previously, living a bachelor's life and enjoying the outdoors and horses, men and public places where lots of people had conversations with him.

Even as he sketched her brows, he wonders if the men who stopped at the previous inn were on their way tracking him down. He tries not to think about them now. However, he also knows he must be always on guard against evil men or women who would stop at nothing to gain a few gold coins.

He looks at Joanne, who is very relaxed, showing off her succulent femininity to Garty.

He has sketched her beautiful brow, golden hair, sleepy, deep blue eyes like a bright night, her white décolletage extending to her young bosoms tucked carefully into her figure hugging dress that seemed to amplify her curves and loveliness.

His mind wandered a little as he struggled to draw her waist.

I would rather draw her to myself, he thinks rashly. *I am sure that my hand spans would meet around her tiny waist. She is a delicate yet robust flower.*

Before he is finished the sketch in charcoal pencil, he feels an eerie coldness washing over him. He looks up to see two horses and a sulky rolling down the narrow way toward the Etty Inn!

What a wonderful dream, he dreamed and now it is all spoiled by what he terms *an intruder*. He must awaken his own suspicious mind once again.

Garty says loudly, "Your brother returns!"

Joanne, is meanwhile slumbering in the ambience of fresh air, birds singing, the aroma of apple blossoms budding profusely, lemonade bubbles on her tongue and in her hair. She almost feels ecstatic at the thought of a beautiful, handsome and talented man drawing her profile.

She has never felt so exotic and sensual in her entire life of twenty years. She knows that this garment made the most of her figure, flattering her to be her wholesome and youthful best. She has even applied a little blush and white powder to her face this morning, just in case they met again.

"Brother," she says, leaping up!

"Get rid of the extra vessels, quickly," she says this as if there might be a fierce fight in a moment over a drinking glass!

"I'm off to my room..." She quickly departs, then returns to collect her small sequinned purse. Garty works swiftly, closing his sketch pad, rushing to the kitchen with one jug and one glass and returns to sit alone, sketching a little brown bird sitting in the tree, picking up bugs.

He detects Jazzon pulling up and being attended to by Sack. He relaxes and tries to enjoy a quiet moment alone. He did have a lot of catching up to do with his notes and information gleaned from his days of interviews. But, it now seems more difficult to concentrate after his encounter with the beautiful Joanne with the narrow waist and ample bosom. In some distant dream he had imagined someone like her in his life. Now that it has happened he had no idea what to do about anything.

Here is her brother, guarding her like a bloodhound guards a fort. My chances of a pursuit of this beautiful lady are slim, he muses.

Jazzon walks past and Garty pretends not to see him, appearing to be absorbed in his notes and sketches.

"Been sketching my sister?" Jazzon asks.

Garty looks at him and is sure that he appears guilty. He tries to appear calm.

Can I lie to this thug? I most certainly can, he thinks, and is about to do so, if Jazzon's interrogation gets nasty.

Chapter 17

"Jesting, my good Sir," Jazzon laughs very heartily, like someone who had been drinking too much rum or wine. Spittle trails from his lips as he brushes his nose with the back of his hand. "You fell for it. Almost!" He says this in a jovial mode.

Garty smiles briefly and continues sketching the brown bird, that has now flown.

"Like a rum, old boy?" He pushes Garty's arm so roughly that his pencil drew a line across the page.

Garty pauses and sucks in a deep breath. Jazzon does not apologise but smirks cheekily.

"No! Thank you Jazzon," Garty says.

"I was about to go to my room..." he says, packing up his few things around the table and exiting.

Jazzon is now busily calling Sack to join him for a rum as the Innkeeper fed the horses and tied up the twin sulky for Jazzon, who was too lazy to do so.

Something about this man stirred an uneasy spirit inside Garty's soul. He was not afraid of Jazzon but he was concerned about what might happen to his sister if he interfered too much in her daily rituals.

At lunch, Garty did not see Joanne or her brother. Also, at the evening meal, they were absent. He called to Madam Etty and asked if everything was okay with the couple?

"I haven't seen them for a time. I did expect some interaction at supper," Garty says, displaying his concern. *I have a genuine concern for Joanne.*

"They prefer their own room service today. I suppose they might be tired after their long journey here?" Madam Etty says, giving this trite reason to Garty as if it was a napkin he needed.

"I see. Very well. I shall dine alone this evening," he tells her.

"Perhaps you shall meet them in the morning when they feel more inclined towards company," she replies, placing a fine dish of vegetables, mainly turnips, on his table, freshly cooked.

I hate turnips! Garty takes a deep breath.

"By the way, Etty, can I settle my account after dinner, pay in advance as well, just in case something eventuates and I need to depart speedily?" he asks politely, putting down his utensils and looking into her broad face.

"Certainly, you may do just that!"

She takes the unused cutlery and extra plates from the table and heads for her hot kitchen.

So, she was expecting them to be at this table! Now I am really concerned.

Garty sits up late into the night, burning the oil lamps, checking out bits of paper with scraps of information he needed to collate. He looks through the sketches he made recently and compared them to the picture of the queen. None seemed a match at this stage. As he looked through the file he had borrowed from the orphanage once again, he took stock of all the details thereupon. He read the entry that was barely legible by now, being years in the files and covered in sticky dust.

He extracts his magnifier and studies each word carefully. The parchment is now becoming more fragile and he is sorry about its dilapidated state. He is sure there remains something in this file that can give him some clue and direction as to where the princess might have gone after being at the orphanage. And then he sees it, the smallest piece of cloth, right at the bottom of the fold in the file. Gently, he picks it up with a small metal tool he bent to pick up minute items. He examines its structure with his magnifier, another practical tool he often uses. Its fibres are scarlet with some golden threads. It is such a tiny piece of cloth that it begins to disintegrate as he touches it. He examines the weave of the cloth, and determines it was possibly made by gypsies. That is such a clue to the existence of the princess that he decides to celebrate, alone.

He finds his way to the pantry and manages to find a jug of ale and a glass. He returns quietly to his quarters, vowing to pay for this extra sustenance on the morrow.

As careful as a man can be, he places the tiny piece of cloth into a small envelope and tucks it in the file. He needs to clarify its maker in the morning, when he can see it more clearly in daylight.

Someone around here may be able to recognise its origin?

Pleased with himself, he undresses and dons his night shirt and long johns, although it was not a cold night. However, if he needed to go in haste, it would save him time, he reckons.

He is about to turn down the oil lamp when he hears a soft knock on his door. He wonders who on earth can be here at this time of night. Taking his pistol in his hand, he keeps it behind his back.

"Who's there?" He asks as quietly as possible. If there is a problem with Brill, it will be one of the Innkeepers. But, he reasons, it is late, after 11:00 PM and he expects them to have gone to their own quarters at this hour because they rise early.

He opens the door a smidgen and knows at once that it is Joanne. Quickly, he opens the door and whisks her inside. She is wearing a glowing blue night dress and carrying a little box in one hand and a dark bottle in the other. Her hair tumbles over her bare neck and onto her shoulders. Garty is taken aback. He looks at her in shock.

"What on earth are you doing here at this time of night? Are you all right?"

"I'm fine," Joanne says, sauntering into his domain. "I thought you might like a bedtime drink," she says, holding up the dark bottle and a glass. "Plum wine," she explains. "Do you have an extra glass here?"

He is concerned that she might attempt to visit the kitchen or dining area of the establishment to find suitable drinking glasses and awaken her brother or the Innkeepers.

"Yes, I have one here." He finds his glass near the table. "I stole this from the pantry," he says lightly.

"Naughty Garty," Joanne chides. She pours plum wine into his glass and into her own glass. She looks into his eyes as he draws closer. Her cheeky grin is magical and he drowns in her eyes. He can barely speak, but must.

"What is going on" he did not finish his thoughts, *inside her head*?

She laughs lightly.

"My bad brother," she begins. She twirls around as she speaks. He watches, fascinated by her movements and the drink in her hand. She does not spill a drop.

"What about your brother?" Garty asks, genuinely concerned, if not for his own welfare, for hers too.

"Asleep! He is sound asleep after drinking a lot of rum. All day long!"

Her eyes drown in his once again! She twirls in front of him again and again.

"I am free," she exclaims, jumping on his partly unmade bed, looking like something he could only imagine was a vision of a ghost in pale blue transparencies leaping around his bed. *A nymph or mermaid without water perhaps, drowning my sorrows,* he is thinking.

"Let us drink to that," Garty suggests tentatively.

Then it happens!

She bounces off the bed and almost falls on her knees, but quickly recovers her composure, and holds her glass high. Garty reaches out and lifts her to her feet. *What or who is this woman?* Garty wonders. *Perhaps she escaped from an asylum? But, no, she is lovely and sane,* he rejects his negativity.

"Thanks for saving me! We drink," she says, standing next to Garty with her hand out to toast his glass.

"This happens to be the world's most expensive plum wine," she adds.

He raises his glass and she joins in, clinking together, making a vibrating sound. "Solid crystal," she mentions the fact.

Garty's mind is in a quandary. He wonders just how solid it should be if they clinked a little too much. *Another bill! I have money now,* he reminds himself.

He feels confused and still doesn't know what her purpose is to enter his boudoir at such a late hour of night. They sup together.

"We must dance," she says suddenly excited at the prospect of dancing again.

"We must?" he asks glibly, pandering to her mood. She empties the contents of her glass in one gulp and places the empty glass on a nearby shelf.

"This is where the music will be streaming," she says. "I brought it with me!" She takes the little box and winds it with a small brass key.

"It is not why I came, but it will do for now," she says in a mysterious tone that fascinates him for a moment.

The music plays and it is joyous, soft and melodious. Garty likes it.

This is sweet music!

He had heard music boxes before but this one is different, ethereal and a little spooky. She holds out her hand and he bows, kisses her hand and they waltz around the room together. He is an awkward untrained dancer and had long ago given up the notion of ever mastering dance steps. *I have two left feet! Now I shall dance?*

She, however, seems adept and flings herself emotionally into the music. He is swept away by her floating movements and his feet seem to be catching on in a very speedy manner.

The music goes on for a long time. They twirl together, come close, move apart, join hands, frolic together a little as their feet keep step with the music playing. Its tune moves from slow tempo to faster and even faster until his head spins with wildness of movement. Then it changes pitch and slows its tempo, so the pair can change their movements and directions at will. It is as if the music has a heart and it is pounding out emotions with every note.

Garty and Joanne are totally infatuated by its tone and power of suspense and do not stop until the music stops.

Garty falls onto the bed, arms and legs akimbo. Joanne falls on top of him. They are exhausted. They look into each others' faces and burst out laughing. It is a belly laugh that keeps them laughing until tears run down their faces.

Her face is a small glow in the lamp light nearby. She seems like someone in a dream. She waits, her face expectant.

"Why did you come here tonight?" Garty stares and waits for her answer. She turns away, looking towards the ceiling. Her chest heaves with exhaustion from the dancing madness.

"The portrait, I wanted to see the portrait," she says, turning her face back to converse.

"You are my portrait," he says softly, with tears filling his eyes.

He leans over and touches her beautiful soft face with its pinkish lips and sleepy eyes. He closes his eyes and gently kissed her soft lips.

This was my dream earlier! She heaves a great sigh and lays her head on his bare shoulder. She senses his strength and safety. Her hair caresses his neck and soothes his senses.

In robot mode Garty rubs one shoulder with his hand. It is slightly stiff. Opening his eyes he sees a shaft of light penetrating the gap in the thick curtaining on his window.

It is early morning. But where is his dream woman, the blue nymph of the night? He feels warmth in the place where she had laid on his shoulder, *but where did she go?* He sits upright and notices the lamp has burned itself out.

He swishes the curtains across in one swift movement with his arms, then stretches his arms high and gazes into the garden through clear glass panels. It is full of light, sun streaking in variegated forms over each flower bed, roses, hydrangeas, daffodils popping yellow heads as if competing with the sunshine.

Chapter 18

Why hadn't he seen these beautiful living things before, he wonders, thumping his chest and feeling like yelling for joy? He listens for a moment. He hears roosters crowing, birds of all kinds whistling as if in a chorus of delight at seeing a new morning. Had his eyes been deceiving him for the light was so bright, beautiful and calming to his soul?

He turns around slowly and sees his manly reflection in the mirror and is surprised to see his strong body naked. A loud knock at the door interrupts his wild thoughts. He hears the voice of the Innkeeper's call. Quickly, he snatches the silk cover from the bed that feels cool and silky on his skin. Gingerly, he opens the door.

"Etty thought you might like some warm water," Sack says in his bland voice.

"Warm water? Of course, thank you for being thoughtful."

"And warm towels," he adds, handing over a bundle of linen, white and bright. "With some face washers," Sack says, pulling a couple of clean wash cloths from somewhere in his long pockets. "And tar soap."

"Thank you kindly."

Garty takes the large jug of hot water and pours it into the basin on the sideboard.

I could do with a nice warm wash and lovely warm towels to add to my joyful morning, he muses.

He sings a song as he washes himself from top to toe with the huge lump of soap. As he washed himself, he feels that he should visit the garden and pick the most beautiful flowering plants and bring them to Miss Weasley in a bouquet of fragrance. He wonders which colours would suit her personality best, pink, red, white, yellow. She is probably sleeping soundly by now, after such an adventurous night that they did not wish to end. Pulling on his clothes over his nicely washed and warm body, he could not stop singing for joy. Entering the garden, he begins to pluck a daffodil when he notices the Innkeeper, Slack, walking past with a bucket of feed. Realising that he should ask permission to snap off the beautiful flowers from their beds, he stops and turns to him.

"I was wondering if I might gather a few of your beautiful blossoms to take to Miss Weasley. I will pay for them, of course," Garty adds, feeling a hot wave sweeping over his face and neck.

Innkeeper Sack stops, holding the bucket aloft. "The Weasley's left, having some urgent matter to attend to..." He chose his words well, and continues, "You see, the sulky is gone and their horse. They left over thirty minutes ago, in great haste! Before I brought you hot water," he adds. He continues walking towards the chicken pen.

Garty stands still, stunned!

"In that case, I shall forego this task and do what I must do immediately," he replies, but the Innkeeper is out of his hearing range.

He dashes inside to grab his cape and hat. Madam Etty walks past at that moment. Garty realises he does not know which way they went? He calls out to her.

"Please, can you tell me which direction the Weasley's drove? I must catch them anon," he says.

"Back to their town, I suppose," she replies, startled at his question as her mind is now on kitchen and cooking. "They live in the Rose

Cottage at Hills Reith," she replies. Then she stops. Her countenance is not a happy one. Her voice becomes low and foreboding.

Garty listens intently.

"Sir, I fear for the young woman. The man was in a frightful state of mind, but they have their rights to leave when they choose to." She stares into Garty's face, desiring some explanation that might give her comfort, but he has none to give but the worst kind of information. She asks her question, "Do you know any other reason why they left?" She waits for Garty to reply.

"I discovered that he was drinking a little too much rum yesterday and was quite stern with his sister. I must go in haste to catch them..." Garty replies, not willing to share any more information to his host.

"I shall return when I am satisfied that Miss Weasley is not in harm's way!"

"Wait," she says, rushing past him and into the kitchen from whence she had come. A few moments later, she reappears with a cloth full of freshly baked scones, based with lumps of melting butter. "You must eat as you go, and I wish you well," she says, piling the food into his arms, cloth and all.

Garty is not keen to eat at this point in time, but accepts the food nevertheless. He may feel hungry later. Now, he must get his horse saddled and head towards Hills' Reith, a place he did notice on his map a few days ago. *It is less than a day's journey,* he reckons.

Shortly after, he leapt on his well watered and fed horse, Brill, who is keen to ride as usual. Garty gently kicks his heels into his ribs and they are off at a good trot.

The sun is rising rapidly and Garty knows that he must take a short cut in order to try and meet them on the boundaries of two roads. As they gallop along, his heart races with anxiety as to what might befall his dear friend who delighted him so much that he can barely breathe thinking of their wild night together. Absorbed in his thoughts and what he might encounter when he meets her brother, he does not notice a caravan of marauders coming towards him in the distance. Before he is able to turn away, they spot him.

He recognises the sulky from Maud's Inn at Scatt a few days ago.

The leader, with his hair flowing behind him and his face intent on finding their prey, shouts.

"That's him!"

A shot is fired at Garty from about 50 yards.

Garty ducks and weaves on Brill, through the nearby trees in order to get away. He sees there are three men and he cannot imagine how he will survive a gun battle out here in the green hills with few thickets. He had considered trying to negotiate with them when they followed after him to the Gypsies camp, but they did not appear friendly, and now seem determined to kill him. He ducks behind his horse's head and whispers to his beast, "Faster Brill, faster," he says, as they gained distance on him. He hears shouts in the distance as bullets whizz right past his ears. He heads towards a small thicket, where there may be a place to hide?

Then it happens. His head strikes a branch on a tree and Garty finds himself flat on the ground. Brill has gone ahead. He shouts to his horse, "Go Brill, go on..." The horse turns back for a moment and then disappears into the nearby thicket. Garty is immediately surrounded by the three men who fired at him. He sits on the ground, winded and sore. Before he can speak, one of the men has his arm around his throat and a pistol at his head. The leader stands above, mocking him. His hair falls across his brow and his leather cape made him appear magnificent and daunting.

Garty recognises him as Black Mack, a notorious bandit who is guilty of causing many serious crimes and known for his treachery. His friends are also notorious bandits, Barley Rock, a man of massive proportions who was once a champion wrestler, chose the path of violence and thievery. The third man, thin and short, Baddy Pin, pale as a ghost, hair like straw, who was a trainee bank teller. Now he is an outlaw of notoriety, the accountant for thieves. Garty knows these three mean business, their reputation being one of brutality and unrivalled success in robbery.

Garty tries to speak, but his chin is locked like a vice by the strong hand of Barley Rock.

"Let him go!" Black Mack speaks in strong language. Barley Rock released his grip reluctantly, squeezing Garty's jaw so much it almost snaps in two.

Garty swallows with difficulty as vague thoughts and vanishing plans about what he can do to save his own life now drift into his head and out again.

Boyhood instincts, long lost in adulthood rear up inside his deepest soul. He needs to find the weak link in the fray, to see a way out of his dilemma. He remembers his pistol is loaded, but now may be used against him. He should have been more careful, quicker and watching more keenly, he chides his mistakes inside his soul. *If I can wiggle a little and grab my pistol cock with my fingers, I can fire at least once and cause a scuttle. I can then run towards the trees and take a chance....*

A steel boot strikes his cheek as his world morphs into blackness.

He wakes to argumentative voices in the distance. At first he thinks: *they are inside my head, demons! I must be in Hell!* Slowly, painfully, he opens his eyes. Everything around him appears blurry. At first his thoughts go awry as to what had just occurred, and when this happened, a few minutes ago or did it happen hours ago? He cannot determine this factor.

I am in excruciating pain.

His chest is hurting so much that he can barely breathe. He stares at his chest and sees it is shirtless. His jacket and cape are gone. He sees his bare legs and his barely covered hips. They left his underwear as it is shabby and useless to thieves with its patches and holes. He feels his cold, bare feet. They took his boots, that were actually not his at all!

His head falls back in despair, and Garty emits a groan. He tries to get to his feet.

"He's not dead!" says Barley Rock, kneeling down and punching him in the face, over and over with his iron fist. Garty swoons and falls back against the tree.

"Enough," the voice of Black Mack is heard. Barley Rock growls as a lion standing over Garty like a champion boxer filled with emotion and strength and ready for another round.

"What do you wish to reveal Mr Garty?" Black Mack asks, also standing over Garty, causing him to try to look upwards at his raging face. His hair fell in tufts onto his leather long coat and jacket. His hat cast a deep shadow over his skin, dark and leathery from years of waiting for victims at noon. His eyes peered into Garty's face, red blurred lines with lines of anger. Fear is creeping over him as the shadow of Black Mack's form covers his torso. The sun is retreating and Garty wishes he had too, before this encounter happened. He tries in vain to sit up but pain causes him to feel faint and weak.

"What do you want from me?" Garty struggles to bring out the words and Black Mack steps back a pace. He sees the damage they have done to their victim. "You've got my clothes, my money, my pistol...what else do you want?" He stuttered the words as his pain waned and then increased to a high point, like waves inside his body. "I am dying..." he adds, tasting blood in his mouth and spitting it painfully away.

"Where is she?" Black Mack asked, leaning towards him again, in case his hearing was dulled. "Can you hear me speaking? I am Black Mack and I am King of Highwaymen here. You are in our territory!"

"Who?" Garty asked, wondering if they were seeking Joanne and her brother for a moment.

"The princess," Black Mack said forcefully, his lips curling and spittle landing on Garty's face. He closes his eyes and tried to shield his face but lifting his arm caused much pain.

"She is invisible!" Garty shouts the words as blood streams from his nose.

"She does not exist!"

"Liar," says Black Mack, becoming furious.

"You have been on this mission for years. We know all about you," he spat again into Garty's bloodied face.

"I have tried to find her but to no avail..." Garty's words trailed away.

It is true, he moaned inwardly.

Black Mack turned to Baddy Pin and Barley Rock.

"So, what lies have you been telling me?"

Chapter 19

He believes me! Finally! I know the truth myself.

They step away from their leader.

"We heard that he found her and was bringing her to the King." Baddy Pin speaks with a jittery voice.

Black Mack shakes his fiery head.

"Looks like you were wrong. One hundred per cent wrong." He heaves a sigh. He turns away from Garty to say his next words.

"We shall needs bring a message to the King's brother, Axemanix and tell him she is no more!" He turns to Garty.

"So, is she dead or alive in your opinion?"

They stare at Garty.

Garty can barely understand the words they speak. His ears are ringing loudly.

"She may be dead already, or never existed..." he says these words from his heart as he has tried in vain to find the princess. "You have the picture, go and find her yourselves!" he says in a moaning voice.

"Picture?" Black Mack asked. "What picture?"

"In my pocket, the jacket you stole from me!"

"Look in his pocket," he snarls.

They try to find the pocket and fumble around the clothes lying on the ground, including Garty's scarlet cape.

"Here it is!" Said Baddy Pin triumphantly.

"Whose picture is this?" Asks Black Mack.

"The Queen, Bianco the Beautiful," says Garty.

Black Mack throws the picture on the ground and stamps on it.

"This is not the princess, you pair of thumping fools," he yells at the pair who looked totally frozen with fear.

"We got the gold," said Baddy Pin. "That's a lot of gold!" He adds.

"We will need to explain everything to Axemanix, and your heads will be on the chopping block. I order you to come up with a better plan, and a live princess! Find one!"

"Yes, Sir, we will!" Said the pair of thieves immediately.

"Come on, let's go and get something to eat. I am famished," said Black Mack. "I think there is an inn near here," he adds.

"What about him?" Barley Rock asks, longing to give Garty another kick and punch. "I have the strength to demolish him, break him in pieces!"

"Leave him be. If he dies, he dies, and if not, then he lives," says Black Mack philosophically.

He is human after all! Garty feels relief.

The pair of thieves shrug their shoulders. They like their master and his words are gospel to them. The three ride away with their sulky and horses as if nothing has happened.

Garty hears their sound for a little while, then silence reigns. He reaches for the little, stamped upon picture and holds it in his hand.

He has lost everything except for his life! *What must I do to stay alive,* he wonders? It is the hardest question he had ever asked himself and he has no answers. *Stay calm!*

He feels cold and shivers constantly. His breathing is becoming worse every time he moves. Feeling exhausted by staying awake, he closes his eyes and drifts into a restless slumber, huddled in the foetal position.

Voices nearby awake Garty. He wonders if the trio returned to finish him off. He lays on the grassy earth. His mouth is filled with blood.

Am I still alive? Horse's hoofs appear near his face that he recognised them at once.

A sigh of relief rushes through his veins.

"Brill!" Garty whispers.

Voices come close and he recognises one voice, Bubba, the young stable strapper from Maud's Inn who took a liking to Brill and the horse reciprocated her kind heart.

Brill and Bubba, he thinks as his emotions overflow with gratitude. *Save me!*

As the sun slowly sets beyond the horizon, his friend's long shadows fell over him as angel's wings. He hears another voice but does not recognise it.

"Hello, can you hear me?" Bubba says, close to his ear. Her hand touches his jugular as she finds a pulse.

"He's alive, but only just," she informs her companion. She leans over Garty, who lay in the foetal position on his side, where his vision is limited to things near the ground. He is barely conscious but blinks with his eyes to signal his recognition of her.

"This is Lad, our newest strapper," she explains. Garty sees the boots of the young man who has long legs, he notices, noting his appearance. *He is young, tall and thin, with sandy hair,* he notes mechanically, as his face looms close.

"Mrs Bouchée has given me her medical kit and we are going to bandage the wounds that are bleeding, so take a sip of this to help you," Bubba says. Her young companion kneels down beside Garty and touches his lips with something that tastes like strong gin or whiskey. Garty feels fluid mingled with blood. He finds himself relaxing a little after that, and it numbs his pain. He is grateful to this pair of unlikely paramedics.

"We think that your ribs are broken, so we will be careful getting you into the sulky." Lad says, examining Garty's wounds. He is not too sure he can survive a jog in a sulky, but there is nothing else they can do. They placed straw on the floor of the sulky to help with its bounce. Garty is relieved to be away from that area where packs of wolves roaming would have surely attacked him, if not, the highwaymen may have returned to finish him off! Either way, he is doomed to die.

They wash his cuts and bruises in oil, and then wrap his wounds. Also, taking care to wrap his ribs with secure bandaging, to keep his bones intact. His head too is split, pouring blood. The pair use all the bandages Mrs Bouchée had given them and all the medication is dried up as well before they move him into the sulky.

With a heave-ho they manage to haul Garty onto the sulky floor. He grimaces with pain, and tries to be brave. Now, he is too weak to scream or shout. Garty cannot even thank the pair. Bubba covers him in a fine light woollen blanket. It keeps the last remnant of his bodily heat intact.

"You all right there, Sir?" Asks Lad as he hops into the sulky driver's seat just in front of Garty's head.

"We have decided to take you to Saint Benedicts hospital. It's closer than the inn and they can help you more than we can."

Garty does not argue.

Bubba leaps on Brill and the little group meander along on quiet, rough paths. Garty knew of St. Benedicts. It was near the orphanage he had visited, so braced himself for a two mile ride on bumpy laneways. He hopes they have pistols to defend their position if they meet highwaymen. He prays semi-lucidly for protection. He drifts in and out of consciousness as they move slowly to the hospital gates. *Will I survive,* he wonders? If so, *I will surely thank these young people for coming to my rescue and give Brill the biggest apple I can find.*

The stench of disinfectant makes his nostrils twitch. Garty tries to open his eyes. They feel glued down! He forces himself to see a little.

He sees through a sliver of sight. He is being transported through a wide hallway and into a room with a very high ceiling. Everything is painted white, which hurts his eyes. They stop.

A male with a white coat and a female in white stand over him. There is also another man in a dark brown habit, with scapular and cowl. He has something in a little jar and pours it into Garty's open mouth. His mouth is being prised open by the nurse and doctor in harmony. Garty gulps the peculiar liquid and swallows in agony. He can smell the product but cannot recall its name. He begins to feel extremely drowsy, even a little merry, as if he had been drinking for a whole week.

In a feverish way he sees Joanne looking into his eyes. He cannot touch her for his arms are heavy and tired. The figure of Joanne speaks with a new voice, a sound like running water. He has a momentary thought that he is levitating, and is now in Heaven. They are together in Heaven, he thinks, frantically trying to work out his surrounds and how they got there?

"We have given you something to ease your pain."

The woman in white moves closer.

Garty looks into her eyes and her face floats before him. He wonders what they have given him and then he sees her big brown eyes. He panics! It is not Joanne! Wrong eyes! They are trying to trick me! But he is in some kind of straight jacket so that he can barely move an inch.

She smiles at Garty and whispers, "You will be fine. Two ribs are fractured in your thoracic cage, and will need time to heal. I am nurse D'ear, This is Doctor O'Manna and our resident chaplain, Padre Byrne."

"The straight-jacket is simply a precaution." The nurse intervenes when she notices panic in Garty's face.

"You will need to be quiet and rest," says Doctor O'Manna, in such a cool and calm voice that Garty relaxes as if under his spell. His face is long and thin, with droopy eyes of steel. He stares into Garty's face and pauses. "It is your lungs that are damaged and cause difficulty breathing. That is why you must be still. It is imperative!"

The doctor and nurse share glances. The Padre blesses him with a large brass cross between his stumpy fingers.

Garty feels defeated and his mind sends him strange messages. Dozing, he is running through long grass following a girl with golden hair wearing a red dress. It is a happy yet frustrating dream. *I cannot catch her!*

The following day he is allowed a warm sup of broth, which tasted salty on his tongue. His mouth has healed quite rapidly and he is able to taste some elements like salt and sugar. He is a little stronger but his breathing has not improved. He still has the straight jacket and is tied to the bed posts, wonders how on earth he can get it off to visit the latrine.

Shortly after 7:00 AM, two burly male orderlies, dressed in white jackets that cannot close over their massive bodies, parade in with a young nurse who has vibrant lips. They work together to untie the straight jacket, held him over a portable latrine, then place the straight jacket back on again and lift him into the bed, tying him to the bed posts. They ask nothing and leave without saying goodbye.

Humiliating! Garty moans.

The room is silent and he is alone. He closes his eyes and dozes off into another dream, where he is still chasing the girl in a red dress. He finally catches up with her and she has turned into a horse. *"Brill,"* he whispers. That makes him happy and he relaxes and sleeps soundly.

By the third day, Garty is feeling much stronger. His head wound has been sutured, is healing and doesn't need bandaging, just a little iodine. He is still in the straight jacket as his breathing is not easy. He is still alone in the room, *probably because of his fever* he decides. He resolves to endure this torture of a kind while he recovers. *I need to recover!*

Ten days later, he is allowed visitors. The warders remove his straight jacket and dress him in a white gown tied with cords. Garty is so relieved that he walks around his room twice when the doctor and nurse leave after their visitation. He is now allowed to eat and drink other foods besides broth, which is also a relief. That very day he has his first visitor since his attack. A voice in the doorway cheers him, but he feels embarrassed while wearing a hospital gown. He sits stiffly in bed and covers himself with the woollen blanket.

"Come in, Bubba," he calls out. She sticks her head in first and smiles at him, then hurries towards the bed. It is a large room for one person and it has a hollow sound when people speak. She walks right up to the bed and pulls up a chair standing nearby for visitors.

Chapter 20

"Lad came too, so we rode safely here," she says in her soft sweet voice.

Lad strides into the room carrying a bundle of clothes. He places them on the second chair in the room.

"I expect you need these," he says with a huge smile.

Garty feels at home with these two.

"Hey, you two, thank you for saving my life!" Lad holds his hand out.

"It is a pleasure to help, Sir. It was Brill who gave us the alarm, otherwise you would have been left on the side of the track ..."

"I know that! I thank you for trusting my dear friend, Brill."

"We love Brill," Bubba says. "He came with us today. Can we bring him in to see you?"

Garty falls back on his pillows collapsing like a rag doll.

"They had me in a straight jacket until today. I think it was actually helping me."

Bubba immediately tries to help plump up his pillow so that he feels secure.

"I see a window there, perhaps we could allow Brill to stick his head in?" She has a cheeky grin on her face. It makes Garty smile. He has hardly ever seen her smiling.

She is such a serious young woman, he thinks. *This is a pleasant change!*

But, be does not feel up to prancing over to the window wearing this inadequate gown that opens at the back view. His face turns red at his own thoughts. *I am too ashamed!*

"You can try some of these clothes on first, if you like?" Lad suggests sensitively.

"Yes, here, this is a shirt, white to go with anything. I hope it is your size?" Bubba says. "And a pair of black breeches," she adds, picking up a thick velvety product on the chair. "With chocolate brown jacket to blend together," Bubba says thoughtfully. "It is also velvet," she says rubbing her hand lightly over the fabric.

"Where did you get these?" Garty asks, totally shocked, sitting up quite straight momentarily. He had lost everything and was at the end of his mind trying to figure out what he should wear when he gets out of here?

"I will help you to get dressed, if you like," Lad says.

"Do you want to get the horse to the window while I help Garty?" Lad asks Bubba, who leaps off the chair and without hesitation, dashes outside to find Brill.

She has given me privacy.

"I am totally grateful to you," Garty says as he leans on Lad to get dressed. It is a little painful, but bearable.

"These are spare clothing at Mrs Bouchée's, and we guessed your size correctly, methinks," says Lad as Garty stands up, holding on to the bed frame for stability.

"We brought boots as well," he says, taking the leather chocolate brown pair in hand.

"These are my old boots, mended," Garty says, shocked.

"Yes, the cobbler brought them to the inn and was asking where you were?"

"That's bad," said Garty.

Lad made a quizzical expression.

"Why so?'

"Because I was wearing the boots he gave me to borrow when I was attacked. I have no idea where they might be!"

"That's unlucky," says Lad. "I am sure someone will need them and they shall reappear one day! Do you wish to wear your old boots?"

He is so positive that Garty feels stronger just talking to Lad.

Garty sits on the edge of the bed and with Lad's help manages to get his old boots on again. He stands up and nods his head in appreciation.

"He has done a great job, they feel just as they did before, even better," he says happily.

"I shall repay the cobbler when I return." He hopes that somehow he can do just that.

Without money I am undone, he thinks, *but faith may shine on me again,* he hopes.

They hear a knock on the glass pane of the window. Lad dashes to the window and finds it welded together, as it had not been opened for years. With brute force he manages to unlock and separate the sash and push it upwards. He can see the horse's nose immediately. The window opening was now almost as big as Brill's head, so the horse, coaxed by Bubba, shoves his face through.

Garty is delighted.

Supported by Lad he comes forward slowly. Lad carries a chair in his other hand and places it near the window, so that Garty can have a chat with Brill.

The pair enjoys a quiet conversation whilst Garty pats Brill's cheeks and muzzle. The horse responds with soft neighs, until someone walks past and shouts at them.

"What are you doing, Miss?"

Garty hears someone address Bubba, who is trying to explain what she is doing.

"It is not hygienic to have a horse in a hospital. Get him out of there immediately or I shall report you to the director," the voice of an older male orderly says with much force. "We won't tolerate that behaviour here," he says with vehemence. His whole face shakes with temper.

"Take him away! Goodbye Brill, we shall meet again," Garty says reluctantly as the horse retreats from the window opening.

I cannot endure another argument.

A week later, Gary enjoys another visit from Bubba, who rides to see him on Brill. He is walking gingerly around and feeling a lot better. His torso is still being bandaged but he knows he is recovering. He is delighted to see Bubba at the door of his room. She has the biggest grin on her face.

She hands him the local newspaper from Scatt.

"You are now officially famous, read the front page," she declares.

Garty is surprised to see a drawing of himself on Brill in monochrome. "Not a bad likeness," he says, chuffed. At first it seems like a noble report, about how he had been attacked and is now recovering at Saint Benedicts, having lost all his possessions.

"Well, that is not entirely true," said Garty to Bubba as she drops her rear on a chair beside his bed. "Because I do have a few things at Etty's Inn, including all my ledgers and some other property!"

"I almost forgot that we found this little picture locked in your hand on that fateful day."

She hands him the little picture of the Queen.

"I am sorry," she adds. "I tried to brush it clean. I think I made it worse! Sorry!"

"Thank you. I was wondering what happened to it." Garty stares at the damaged little picture and places it on the small table near his bed.

"I still don't know why Madam Etty hasn't sent your belongings here to you?" Bubba says, looking into Garty's face with a quizzical expression.

"Because they have no idea what happened to me, I suppose. Who would tell them about this? They are rather isolated, you know," Garty says in a thoughtful fashion. "I must get back there and explain my disappearance. They know I was looking for the Weasley's, that's all."

"We should have visited there and collected your things," said Bubba. "We have been neglectful," she says in response. She looks sad.

"Quite the contrary, Bubba! Please don't be sad. You have done admirably." Garty speaks softly to her and pauses before he continues. He wonders with whom she came today, as it is a treacherous route here.

"Did you come alone today?" Garty asks Bubba. He looks out for Lad, but he is missing.

"Lad had too much to do and I felt it was necessary to come and bring Brill once again, and I brought you some other things," she adds excitedly.

"Other things?" Garty questions wondering what on earth she is so excited about.

"This notice in the newspaper, published by Mr Jael, has created quite a lot of excitement in our town. People have been coming to the inn to give you gifts of gold and other items, because you lost everything in the attack."

She hands over a large saddle bag carried on Brill's back. Garty takes the bag into his hands and now almost speechless, opens it. He shakes his head and feels emotional as he sees many needed items, including a velvet jacket.

"And this gold," says Bubba, handing over a small velvet bag she has also carried on the journey.

"You will be able to survive for some time, I imagine."

Garty is dismayed that she has carried money safely with so many highwaymen about.

"Bubba, I am almost speechless, but thank you," Garty says, withholding tears. "Please tell the folk in Scatt how thankful I am?"

"I shall," she replies happily, bubbling over with delight. Bubba leans over and gives him a gentle hug, remembering his injuries. He responds by holding her close for a moment.

She smells of the outdoors, roses and apples, he thinks.

"Keep the saddle bag for when you leave here," she suggests.

"Thank you! This is unbelievable, the generosity of the townsfolk! I could not have dreamed they cared so well!"

There was enough gold to pay for any medical bills and also for Brill's care.

"Here, you must take these for Mrs Bouchée, in thanks for taking care of Brill."

"I shall do so," said Bubba, accepting two gold coins.

"Now, I shall open the window and allow Brill to enjoy a tete-a-tete with you!"

An hour later, Garty bade goodbye to his horse and Bubba, reluctantly, but he was also tired now.

"We will return tomorrow," she shouts, waving her hand as her hair blew in the afternoon breeze. *She is so lovely,* Garty thinks. *A gem not to be lost,* he mused.

On the following day, the doctor reluctantly agrees to allow Garty to discharge from Saint Benedicts.

"You must however promise to rest for another week or two before you return to working at full pace," the doctor commands.

Garty simply nods.

"I shall do my best to rest and recover," he says, *I cannot allow Bubba to keep riding alone to see him on that treacherous pathway. I must return to my work.*

Garty packs his things and wonders if he should ask to hire a horse and buggy locally, to return to Etty's Inn, where he can still rest and recuperate, obeying the doctor's orders.

While he is wondering what to do about his travel, he hears a noise at the window. He flings open the window, now nicknames Brill's window.

What a shock to see his faithful horse Brill, who is happy to see his master. Happiness washes over him on seeing her horse, but something seems amiss?

"What are you doing here?" Asks Garty, wondering: *does the horse know that I am being discharged from Saint Benedicts? Now I am acting as if a horse has insight and intuition,* Garty thinks wryly.

Garty's happiness plummets from happy to curiosity in a moment.

"Wait on, who rode here?"

He heads outside to check Brill and finds scuff marks on his back. The saddlebag is gone. He picks up a piece of green cloth fibres in one of the chains attached to the reins. His heart melts.

Garty gathers his things and quickly informs the sister that he must leave immediately.

Chapter 21

She chases him with a bundle of papers to sign. He scribbles his signature speedily, his heart thumping with anxiety.

"Are you sure you are well enough to leave?" Sister Mona asks.

"I must leave, for it is imperative," he replies. "Please give my thanks to the staff and doctors here."

She watches him leave on his faithful horse, and shakes her head.

"Men, they are forever restless," Sister Mona says quietly. She assumes he is leaving because of some broken hearted female waiting for his return. She is sceptical of all men!

Garty rides at a trot. He feels comfortable in his chest at this rate, so is pleased with their progress. He follows the track he believes Bubba may have travelled and keeps an eye out for any signs of a struggle. The track is overgrown with trees and bush so that he finds nothing of suspicion. He stops a couple of times to check on sounds, but these are simply birds singing in the treetops.

He reaches the Maud before noon. Maud Bouchée is shocked to see him walking through her door. She is busy at her desk and looks over her glasses at him as if she has seen a ghost. She almost faints as she holds onto the counter and takes a few deep breaths. She quickly comes around the counter and holds him as a lost son, with tears in her eyes.

Garty feels quite embarrassed at this gesture. His heart is thumping wildly and he feels a few jabs of pain across his chest.

"Thank you for sending those medical supplies. They saved my life!"

"Come and sit down," says Mrs Bouchée. "We thought you were fallen," she says in a hushed tone. There is no-one in the reception room of the inn and the places for lunch are already set.

"What else should a body have done for someone who is like a son to me?"

She stares at him as if she is his mother.

Garty sits down, almost overwhelmed by her reception. He would never have believed she felt this way about him until this happened.

"Something to drink!" She yodels as she quickly rushes away and returns with a large glass of apple juice.

"Get this into you, for you look as weak as water," she exclaims. "Are you recovered so quickly?" Mrs Bouchée asks.

"Mrs Bouchée, thank you for your concern. I am almost completely healed from my wounds," he says smiling as sweetly as he can.

"You sent Bubba to me today, I believe?"

"I did indeed! She was up before the crack of dawn and completed all her chores, so I asked her to visit you at St. Benedicts again. We collected more funds from locals, so I wanted you to have them straight away of course!"

"Well, she did not get to Saint Benedicts," he replies dourly.

Mrs Bouchée's face turns snow white in an instant. She clutches the back of a chair and tumbles into it. She puts her face in her hands.

"Dearest Lord, no!" She looks at Garty? "What happened to her?" She asks in a breathy voice. Garty shakes his head.

"I have an idea but it needs a posse of searchers to find out if she was taken?"

"Who on earth would take a young woman on a horse, on a mercy mission?" She speaks as if Garty is not present. "But pray tell me, how do you know all this if you are not a witness?" She asks suddenly. "How did you get here?" She asks two questions at once, as her mind fills with conclusions to the mystery of the missing Bubba.

"I believe she was followed and fell off Brill at some point. I took care on the way here to note any disturbances in the trees or bushes, but it was pointless, nothing was visible to my eyes."

He drains the last of his apple juice and shudders.

"I fear for her life," he says at last. His face is ashen as he looks into Mrs. Bouchée's countenance. They stare into each others eyes for a moment. Both feel devastated and understand each other perfectly.

"She is my charge," says Mrs Bouchée at last. "Bubba is as a daughter to me since I fostered her. We will search until we find her," she exclaims, forming her plan.

"I believe it may be the men that stayed here when you left. They asked strange questions about you and stole some of my silverware," she says, banging the table with her palm. "They will pay!"

Garty watches her, visibly distraught. He too is straining to think of a plan and now to find a resolution for his chest pain that has returned in vengeance. He tries to steady his breathing but it feels as if he has a tourniquet around his chest.

"Now, you must rest a tad for thou seems to be hurting," she says unexpectedly returning to Garty. "I have a great tonic I shall minister to you, but do not say a word about this drop."

She heads into the kitchen and after a few minutes returns with a small measure of a liquid in a vial.

"Drink and say naught."

Garty drinks as instructed.

"This tastes like something I have drunk before…" He can still feel the pain but after a few minutes it seems dulled a little. "It is working," he says, quite surprised. "You should give this recipe to Saint Benedicts," he adds coyly.

"That is where it came from," she says and her mouth tweaks into a smile. "And I did give some to Bubba and Lad to take to you with other supplies as you already know."

She sounded as if she was now finished with this topic, so Garty remained quiet. He did not wish to upset someone who was now becoming his ally in a mission of necessity.

"We shall begin by taking a picture of the young lady and posting it around the region," Mrs Bouchée says. "Also, we shall ask for a newspaper advertisement."

"I have a hand-drawn picture of Bubba," says Garty. "It is at Etty's place!"

Mrs Bouchée looks aghast.

"We can ask Ted to visit there and to bring it here," she suggests.

Garty coughs and squirms in his facial features.

"Is that a problem?" she asks.

"No, no, I am being pedantic, but I would prefer to ask Lad!"

Mrs Bouchée shrugs her shoulders. He was hiding something from her, she senses. But, now that they needed to work together she did not argue.

"We can ask Lad?"

"Thanks. I would prefer that. Also, if he could bring my files, stored in a cupboard in the room, I will ask no more."

"My sister must be out of her mind wondering what on earth happened to you! I shall send Lad as soon as I can," Mrs Bouchée says, dashing off through the wooden doors as if she can wait no longer to put her plan into action.

Garty began to feel so exhausted that he was minded to ask for a bed to rest properly as his breath came with gasps. His pain is inflamed by the thought that Bubba may have been taken captive and she is now his priority. He needed to find her and to bring her home. He closed his eyes and lay his elbows on the table with his hands on his forehead.

"Come on, we've got you!"

Garty hears the words as if he is in a dream. His chin is siting on his Adam's Apple, and his arms are being lifted by two men. Vaguely he recognises their voices.

"Sorry," he hears his own voice utter these words.

"We can take him in here and he can lie down for a time," says Mrs Bouchée in a full fluster. "I should nay have left him in this state!"

"Lay him down there, careful," she says as Garty feels a hard edge under his legs. A bed! He lay on his side and a rug is placed over him. His eyes refuse to open.

"I shall call the doctor," says Mrs Bouchée. "You two get on with the plan," she says to the two fellows who helped him to the room.

It seems like a few minutes before Garty wakes up to find himself in a room he does not recognise. He sees a jug on a small table nearby. There is also an empty vial. He picks up the vial and sniffs.

"Opium," he says aloud. He knows that he had a visit from someone who gave him something to drink. He tries to sit up and calls out, "Mrs Bouchée, Lad!" His voice is a little weak but the words are clear enough if someone is nearby.

"Hey, how are you?" Ted comes through the door. "We found you in a sad state and had to call the doctor," he says, coming right over to Garty and standing over him as he lay on the bed.

"Can you please help me up and fetch me a drink of water?" Garty asks. His pain was lessened, probably by the medicine.

"Surely," says Ted. He heads off to the kitchen and returns with a drink in a cup. "Here you are. Doctor said you should rest for a few days," he adds mechanically.

"A few days?" Repeats Garty, exasperated. "No, I must look for Bubba before something terrible happens to her," he replies.

"Nothing will happen to her, just rest a while," says Ted comfortingly.

Garty's head is spinning and he takes a few deep breaths to get his bearing. "Where's Mrs Bouchée?" He asks.

"She's around somewhere, shall I go and find her?" He asks politely.

"Yes, please," replies Garty. He really wants to know what her plan is for rescuing Bubba. He does not feel confident in discussing the details with Ted. Garty rests his head on the pillow behind his head. He does not hear Ted return with a drink.

"Drink up now. We were all worried about you." Garty hears a click as Ted shuts the door.

"In a moment," Garty mumbles, moving and sitting on the edge of the bed with his feet on the floor. The floor moves even as he stares at it, making him feel nauseous. He sucks a deeper breath, closes his eyes and opens them again. "That's better," he mumbles. *At least the floor has stopped swaying.*

He had not failed to notice that something is amiss in this household. Why did Ted bring him a cup of apple juice and not water? Mrs Bouchée always kept cold water on the stone in the kitchen. Still a little unsteady, Garty heads towards the door, finding his balance at the same time. He presses the door handle and it does not open.

"What? Locked?" He says aloud. *Why would Ted lock the door?* He knocks on the door and calls out, "Hello, anyone there? The door is locked!" Surely Ted is not stupid?

How on earth can I get out of this room, he wonders? There is no window, just this door as an entry point. It is some sort of storage room with a bed and cupboards. He feels improved by the moment as his anger mounts, overcoming his dizziness by default.

The fireplace is open and he looks up the chimney but hesitates about leaving through there! He cannot see any light and it needs the services of a chimney sweeper. *It is too dark up there!* If he was ten years of age he might stand a chance of climbing up there, but now it is hopeless. I am *not fit enough, or thin enough, and would definitely get stuck somewhere in there. Perish the thought. I must find a reasonable way out! Was someone trying to keep me locked away? Why was Mrs Bouchée not bustling about?*

Garty looks around for something long and sharp. He opens old jammed wooden cupboards filled with bits and bobs. *Maybe there is a craft kit somewhere?* Finally he uncovers a small box with hat pins inside.

Just the ticket to freedom, maybe!

Chapter 22

He flops down near the door and begins to figure out the mechanics of the lock. His eyes are usually super sharp but now everything appears a little blurry. He toggles the mechanisms of the lock. Time passes as he twists and turns the hatpin. Finally, he hears a click. He gets to his feet and holds the wall nearby for a moment to steady himself. The door opens. For an instant he barely believes his luck.

Success, hallelujah!

He runs his hands over his perspiration covered face. Gingerly he pulls the door inwards and slides through, closing the door behind him silently. He walks quietly through the small corridor towards the main reception room. His heart is thumping madly as he moves gingerly.

He senses danger may be lurking, not because of his recovery progress but because *there is a spy living here!*

He walks into the reception room and Ellie, Mrs Bouchée's casual helper is near the counter, wearing her new outfit, yellow bonnet and long sleeved shirt over a black pinafore covering a black full skirt.

He approves deeply and instantly wishes to whisk her into his arms and float away. But that is stupid!

"Is Mrs Bouchée around?" Garty asks.

Ellie is surprised to see him and turns abruptly. Her skirt swings as though captured by a delicate easterly tornado.

"No, Sir Garty, Madam has gone to the aid of one of our guests, who claims she was pushed down the steps. Mrs Bouchée is taking care of her in her room." She looks at Garty and her face displays anxiety.

"What is wrong?" Garty asks the frazzled woman.

"Everything is wrong! The buggy has a wheel fallen off one of the horses lost a shoe and now this!" She flings her arms around.

"Everyone is in distress!" She cries out in a weepy voice.

"What about Bubba?" Garty ventures to ask amid the dilemmas happening around about.

Ellie shrugs her shoulders.

"No idea, everyone is rushing back and forth like sea saws..."

Garty is distracted, noticing freshly made sandwiches on a tray nearby.

"Could I please have these, I shall pay," he asks.

"What?" Ellie speaks in a distressed voice. "Those? Someone left them here, take them," she says definitively. She is in a turmoil in her head.

Garty is hungry, so starts to eat greedily.

Ellie looks at him and he stares into her face, munching.

"Sir, I am sorry, do you need a drink?"

She rushes towards the kitchen and returns with a large glass of juice.

"Would you like some apple fresh?" She asks.

"I would, thank you," Garty replies, taking the glass from her and downing it thirstily.

She watches in amazement.

"You were very thirsty," she says at last.

"I have a journey to undertake," he replies, taking the last sandwich in his hands. "I will return as soon as possible."

"I shall tell Mrs Bouchée then, shall I?"

"Don't say anything to anyone. It's not their business," he replies, reflecting on the foregoing events of his being locked in the store room and how Mrs Bouchée did not turn up. As far as he is concerned, *everyone not present is now under suspicion.* Garty dashes around the side of the building and finds Brill nibbling at some hay in a feeder.

"Take a good drink now friend, for we are going on a journey," he says, taking the reins and leading the horse to water.

Someone had released the horse's rope and that is a curiously strange act! Brill is a faithful animal who stayed until now. He pats his neck in thanks. The horse seems to understand and drinks for a minute or two as Garty checks the bridle and other straps to ensure they have not been loosened.

His heart is hammering so fast that he has to take a deep breath to reduce its pace. He checks Brill's shoes to ensure they are in good shape too. He is immediately happy with everything and wonders if he simply forgot to tie the horse up?

Garty is feeling surprisingly vibrant after eating and drinking. He now feels ready to do a search for Bubba, no matter who joins in. He understands that her disappearance is likely to be the fiends who bashed him up and took his wealth, leaving him for dead! He has anxiety raging for Bubba. She is so tiny and vulnerable, he recalls. But, her agility and fine mind can see her through any difficulty.

"We must hurry," he told his horse as he climbed on his back carefully and settled into the saddle. He takes a few deep breaths to check his pain level and it has subsided quite a lot.

"I am ready. Are you ready, Brill?" He asks his faithful horse.

The horse neighs.

He looks around.

Ellie is watching at the back entrance and gives him a nervous wave. He cannot see Mrs Bouchée, but he also cannot wait a moment longer. He notices a few folk walking in the street but he turns towards the opposite direction. He can trust no one here! Garty tries to visualise where the three highwaymen attacked him, and reminds himself of his hand drawn map. He has left it at Etty's when he rushed after Joanne and her brother.

He makes a decision to ride to Etty's and check the map first. Also, he does not have a weapon now and he needed to get one. He rides softly out of town as if he is in no hurry for he knowns that folk love to gossip. He has lost his hat with the red feather and his scarlet cape, which he misses very much. Now he is wearing more ordinary clothing, brown velvet jacket and pants with a very white shirt that is a little tight around his broad, and still aching chest.

This is cleaner than my old shirt, he reminds himself, *and it is fine. I shall suffer these insufferable clothes!*

When they reach the crossroads he looks around to ensure that nobody is watching the rider on a horse. He urges Brill to turn to the left and to head down the old laneway with plenty of foliage for covering.

Garty rides zig-zag through the less used route as he tries to dissuade trackers, keeping his eyes peeled for any unusual activity. This action did cause him a little dizziness, but it was minor and worth the safety aspect. He is getting to know these pathways well, and it pleases him as he ducks to avoid overhanging branches and cautiously traverses muddy dips that might harm or cause his horse to slip and fall. It has been raining the night before and the ground is soft and clumpy in places, but Brill handles it with ease. He pats his horse's neck several times, encouraging him to ride as fast as possible.

Along the track, Garty notices recent equine footprints and buggy wheel prints that present him with an opportunity to consider the area as one in which there had been a scuffle recently.

Dismounting his steed he finds a few sticks, stuck them crossways in the soil marking the spot for more investigation. As soon as he mounts again, he notices smoke in the distance and within a short trot the chimney of Etty's Inn is visible!

Good, someone is at home. He says to his horse, Brill, "Giddy up!"

The horse canters to the inn as if he did it every day in a parade.

"Good boy," says Garty, slipping from his horse and tying him up near a nice patch of grass, green and wet from the refreshing rain. His pain had decreased and he sucked in the freshness of the air greedily. He felt stronger.

Before he entered the reception area, Garty is met by Madam Etty herself. "There you are," she says, behaving as a scolding mother with a naughty child.

"I am here and I am sorry for any worry that I caused!" Garty says, smiling his familiar smile. Etty came right up to him, holding onto the small tool in her hands.

"You are a sight for sore eyes," she says hugging him relentlessly, not releasing the tool in her hand. Garty is worried for a moment that she might give him a smack for being bad. She steps back and he sees her eyes reflecting his face, with tears of joy.

"Where have ye been?" She asks the question with concern as she shrugs her shoulders. "The last thing we know is that you went off to find the

Weasleys and then you vanished," she says passionately.

"I know. I am sorry that I did not get back to you, but I was mugged and left for dead! I am lucky to be alive!"

"What?" Etty says, as her arm drops, still holding her tool. She turns her head towards the back of the establishment and calls out.

"Sack, come here, Garty's back," she says in a very loud voice.

A mumbled sound echoes a reply.

"It must be time for a celebration and you can tell us all about it," she says, tucking the tool in her apron pocket and hurrying softly towards the back of the building. "We will take a sup and enjoy your tale at the rear," she says, glancing back at Garty, who is in a fix between rushing away and not staying a moment too long.

Garty does sit down to enjoy a fresh cup of tea and some of Etty's overcooked scones with lashings of freshly whipped cream and home made gooseberry jam.

"We kept your room, just in case you needed it in a hurry," she says. "We do have another guest here, so everything is financial." Etty explains this secret fact while the Innkeeper enjoys the remainder of scones, cream and jam.

"She's a great cook, our Etty," he keeps saying over and over as he devours the food.

Garty inspects his previous room and is relieved to see everything just as he left it. As soon as he can get his things together, he catches up with Madam Etty in the dining room. She is busily placing new flowers in vases, humming an unknown tune.

"Are you staying for supper?" she asks, brushing past him, giving him a motherly glance.

"I have to go perhaps for a few days, but I feel it is prudent that I pay you in advance," Garty says, holding out several gold coins that are gratefully accepted by Madam Etty.

"That is sufficient for a whole week," she says. "And I do appreciate your custom, and good company," she adds. She did not ask about his business that he seems keen to undertake, but continues bustling about with candelabra dusting, polishing and humming.

Later, she calls Garty as he heads out to mount his horse.

"I want to give you a picnic basket for your hunger," she said. "We also included a bottle of the Master's own brewed plum wine," she says as she happily parts with a tied up in linen hamper.

"Thank you, it is sufficient," Garty says, taking the hamper with him on his steed. He smells the meat as he tied it up to his horse and wishes that he did not have such urgent and important business and could simply enjoy a picnic.

Where can I get the most up to date information about Axemanix's men, and heinous plots?

Before he pats the horse and urges him onwards the revelation comes to him.

About one hour later he rides into the gypsy campsite. He is met at first by a number of men with rifles and other arms.

"Hey, I come in peace," he says playfully, hoping they calm down.

"Of course, you are the friend of our seer, Janda," they say as they move close to Garty and his horse.

"And of Crystalina!" Garty adds, remembering that astonishing woman with eyes like crystal balls and her horsemanship that is to his thinking, absolute perfection.

"She is here too," says the man with a reddish beard standing before Garty holding a rifle. His face is so weather-beaten that he looks at least one hundred years of age.

"Over there,' he declares, pointing in the direction of the caravans. Garty looks in that direction and notices the wonderful young woman again. Her hair shines with the slightest light of the sun and her face is akin to something he can only imagine, *a perfection in beauty desired by all women and loved by all men, especially a man like me!*

She notices him looking her way and responds with a wave of her slim and beautiful arm. She is dressed in a royal blue garment that display her unbelievably pale skin and rosy red lips. Garty stares, fascinated for a moment.

"Are ye blind?" The man with the reddish beard says, mocking Garty.

"Thank you, no, I shall meet with her then?"

He asks the question but also makes it a statement as he rides over there.

The man nods and leaves the scene, quietening other men who also hold rifles. They relinquish their weapons and return to their previous activities.

"Hello," Garty calls out to Crystalina who turns on the little landing area of the caravan. He gasps at her beauty and stares at her. She looks down at him from her high position and smiles. How were her teeth so white and her face so pure? He wonders if she might be an angel from another place and not from this earth?

"Do you wish to see Mother?" She asks this with a twist of her rosy lips.

Chapter 23

Her breath made her perfectly carved breasts rise and fall before his mesmerised eyes. Her dress is styled to charm admirers, especially men, and to provoke envy from females. Her hair is piled on her head, yet many silken tresses fall on her white décolleté.

Garty can barely speak for a moment. He looks at his horse's mane and knows he must fulfil his mission and gain her favour. He looks up at her again.

"Can you please help me?" He asks.

Before she replies, Crystalina has leapt down from the platform as if it is merely a foot high, not six feet! She is limber and light of foot and keen of eye as she stands before Brill and himself.

"You want a deal?" She asks him.

He knows she is a canny person who can take money at a whim, but now someone's life is at stake he must pursue his mission with fervour and intelligence, not lust and passion for her.

"I need to find a missing person," he says as she moves close. He can look right into her spell binding eyes and he withholds a gasp. She knows she is able to control this man who has a multitude of weaknesses in her mind, like every man.

She tosses her hair and breathes heavily, trying to heave her petit bosoms so that he might lose his train of thought.

Garty fights the desire to take her in his arms and kiss her ripe red lips and bosom. *I must keep my head.* Bubba's life is at stake now! He slid easily from his steed and stood next to his beast and faces Crystalina, who looks at him with lowered eyes, eyelashes that shade her eyes, making her even more fascinating. She licks her lips and he drools with desire for her touch, but resists with great determination.

"I need to find the men who work for Axamanix very soon, for they have captured a young woman..."

Crystalina stalks him, looking him up and down, flashing her lashes, protruding her beautifully formed breasts at every opportunity before speaking.

"What's in it for us? We are of one blood here," she adds dramatically.

"I have a plan," Garty begins.

"A plan?" She moves so close he feels her fresh breath, a tang of bergamot.

Very enticing, he muses.

"You are my plan!" Garty says in a stilted voice. He stares into her crystal ball eyes and bears his soul to her.

She is left openmouthed. He turns his gaze away.

"I shall pay your tribe well."

Garty clinches the deal with his offer of gold.

She makes him wait a few moments to enjoy this painful pause.

"I shall do it," she says at last.

He is satisfied. *Gold answers to everything!*

"I shall have to consult Mother,' she says bluntly.

"I am sure she shall agree when I explain the circumstances to her," Garty says.

It seems that evening has come suddenly and the camp fires are beginning to blaze with heat.

"You must not refuse our hospitality," Janda says as Garty wonders what to do next.

The aroma of rabbits cooking and trout grilling are too much to bear for Garty. He is willing to stay and eat with this gypsy band, gladly.

"I will join you, friend," he says to Janda.

He seats himself next to Crystalina and her mother as they eat around the campfire.

It is a pleasant experience, eating and drinking something unidentifiable to Garty, but delightful.

"What is this drink?" He eventually asks Janda, who is watching everyone and everything with extreme interest. Her eyes are similar to Crystalina, dark and piercing, as if she can see inside a person's soul.

"Haw-berry wine," she says, smiling in a way that Garty found disturbing to his deepest manhood.

"It is very sweet," says Garty, belching wildly.

The women on either side of him simply laugh heartily, so much that they almost fall off their humble log seats.

Garty wonders what affect this wine may have on his good judgement, but for a moment in time, feels the sway of dance, the rhythm of music as the flutes play, the banjos play and guitars are strung, amid fire and flame, wine and friends. He feels very much at home.

"I must find Bubba, taken by Axemaniz's men," says Garty at last to Janda, who looks him in the face. She becomes serious for a moment in time. A moment of anger floods her dark eyes.

"We shall find her, and do our best to defeat Axamanix and his allies, for we are foes,' she says dramatically.

"Thank you!" Garty replies, grateful for her support and all the clan with her.

"May we persuade you to stay overnight and we shall commence our search tomorrow?" Janda asks, seemingly ignorant of whatever might befall Bubba before morning.

Garty wanted to think a little more about this matter. He needed to find Bubba as soon as possible, but knows that everyone in his present family need a good night's sleep before commencement of a tryst with foes. He has no option but to agree to Janda and her already half-drunk daughter, Crystalina.

"The night is upon us and we must rest," says Janda dramatically, staring into the skies, overcast with clouds and a seldom peeking new moon. Garty stares into space and falls backwards, groaning.

"You must rest a little, sleep with our tribe overnight, for we are with you," says Janda, decisively.

Garty replies "Yes," without resistance.

He lays on the ground near the fire that is slowly diminishing as its embers turn to ash. He is very tired, his pain is returning despite too much wine. He thinks of Bubba, struggling with the men of vice and he trembles.

She saved my life, now I must save hers!

He lay in the grass, dry from the fire's licking flame, and closed his eyes.

"Here!" The hypnotic voice of Crystalina speaks into his ear.

Garty wakes up from a shallow slumber. He did feel the cold and is grateful for the blanket of wool thrown over his weary limbs. He feels a breath on his face. He opens his eyes.

"I am cold too," says Crystalina.

She pulls a corner of his blanket over her fine arms that are bare. He reaches out and draws her closer to him.

"Warm up next to me," he says. He barely believes what he is doing and saying to this woman who is too beautiful for a man to imagine. She snuggles close to him. He inhales the aroma of her thick and lavish hair, glowing blue in the firelight and feels utmost satisfaction. *I am a lucky man,* he thinks. He pulls her closer.

"Are you looking for a princess?"

Her words speak into his ear. His foggy mind is clearing.

"I am searching for a princess, and now for a missing young woman," he explains in no rational way. His words sound convoluted when spoken aloud, even his quiet whispering.

"The invisible princess?" Says Crystalina, opening her eyes, staring into his in the shadows and flicker of fire.

He stares into her mesmerising eyes. *She is goading me.*

"That is my commission and I shall complete it," he says. Though he now suddenly feels weary in this mission.

She recognises my feelings, he thinks, *like some mystic.* He is content with her strange company.

He kisses her forehead as a father would a child. *That felt impulsive.*

He tries to remain calm and rational, but it was becoming absurdly difficult. He desired to ravish her beautiful body.

Then she spoke.

"Could I be the princess?" She asks Garty, unexpectedly. His eyes open wide. He has never considered Crystalina as the princess!

"No, I doubt it very much!" He mumbled at last. Crystalina responds to his words by slapping him on his bicep.

"Ouch, that hurt!" He rubbed his arm. His chest hurt.

"Why not?" Crystalina asks. He detects anger in her voice. He is scared for a moment. Then he remembered why she cannot be the princess.

"Because you do not look like her," he explains in as few words as necessary.

"What do you mean?" she asks vehemently.

She is worrying him so much now that he wonders if her family might kick him out of their campsite immediately.

"Be quiet," he whispers, trying to calm her voice down. He searches for the picture of the queen in his pocket. Finally he retrieves it and shows it to her. She snatches it from his hands and holds it closer to the glimmer of fire still glowing in its embers.

"This? Who is this?"

"It is the queen," he says. His eyes are open now and he is immediately sober in mind and heart.

"The queen?" She asks the question. "You said you were looking for a princess, not a queen," Crystalina says, her voice puzzled.

"That's true, it's the queen, her mother," he explains. She looks deeply into his eyes now, confronting him fiercely.

"Do I look like my mother, Janda?" She asks defensively. Garty is taken aback and cannot answer her.

As if they have startled Janda in her nightly routine, her voice echoes across the encampment.

"Crystalina, where are you?" Janda calls out.

Crystalina leans over and kisses Garty on the mouth fiercely so that his lips ache.

"I am the princess," she says, rising, brushing her silken dress down and disappearing into the shadows before she answers her mother's call.

"Here Mamma," she says, after a couple of minutes.

The figure of Janda moves as a shadow does and she disappears into the caravan bedroom as Crystalina leaps up to where her mother stood a few minutes before.

Garty snuggles beneath his blanket and falls into a fitful sleep, wondering what to do about his feelings for Crystalina, sensing subtle dangers. Garty is grateful to her mother for calling her away. Now he can rest and refresh his plan to save dear little Bubba!

Breakfast is an informal affair with the gypsies gathering around and lighting a fire. Cooking all sorts of game comes next and Garty watches from around the edges of the campsite. Finally he has an opportunity to speak with Janda about the mission in hand. They have already enjoyed a sumptuous breakfast of roasted fowl and chestnuts, along with delicious sugary treats and breads.

"That was very nice, thank you," Garty says to Janda as they finish up the food and clear the mess, rapidly burning everything unnecessary that is left behind, with the good bits given to the dogs.

"We like to keep the place clean," says Janda, taking out a pipe and smoking a very aromatic burn.

Garty watches and observes that Cyrstalina does not come for breakfast.

"Where's your daughter?" He asks, a trifle worried. "I hope she's not upset about anything?" He asks, carefully choosing his words.

"Why would she be upset?" Janda asks, then continues with her own thoughts.

"Crystalina is just lazy, that's what's wrong with her!"

"I see." Garty replies tentatively, hoping she does not ask about anything that occurred last night. He licks his dry lips.

"I need help to find a young woman," he says, as he stares at Janda. She sucks her pipe, squinting her eyes as she stares at him.

Chapter 24

"Who?" She asks casually. "You looking for that baby princess once more?"

"No, someone else has been taken. Bubba, a stable Strapper who works with Mrs Bouchée!"

"When did it happen?" She looks concerned and places her pipe on a tin plate at her side.

"A few days ago she was coming to Saint Benedicts to bring me supplies when she disappeared. The horse came alone..."

"I see," she says, picking up her pipe and banging it on a log next to the tin plate.

"Have you seen or heard anything around here?" Garty asks.

"I'm thinking, so don't interrupt me," she says in a stern voice. Janda stares into space for a moment, pulling her embroidered shawl around her shoulders as if she felt cold.

"I may know the whereabouts of bandits who do such terrible things," she says at last. "I shall take some time out now."

She gets up without another word, opens her caravan door and enters quietly.

"Get up you lazy thing," she calls out to Crystalina, who replies with a curse to her mother.

Garty hears a bang and a screech and then it is quiet.

Gunshot? Rising, he runs to the door and it is ajar. Cautiously, he pushes it with the palm of one hand, keeping his back to the door. He steps away again as he sees the naked figure of Crystalina, bathing herself with a jug of water and a multicoloured cloth.

"What are you doing?" Janda's voice startles him. She is wearing her black veil and holds her crystal ball. She has sneaked up on him.

"Take your eyes off my child, Sir," she orders. Garty feels the heat rising into his face and head.

"I do apologise, but I heard noises," he explains.

"That was nothing! This is our life and this is our way! Now, please leave me for five minutes," she asks. Her eyes are like fire behind the black lace.

Garty retreats quickly, finding work to do chopping tree branches with the menfolk whilst Janda has some peace and quiet to consult her crystal ball.

Crystalina enjoys her morning toilette.

Garty is becoming a little anxious, when Janda calls out to him. He drops the work with the saw and axe promptly.

"Go on, get your self sorted out," Roma, the red bearded gypsy shouts to Garty and the others nod agreeably.

"I see you are hurting already anyway, and we don't need half a man on this job," he says in a jovial fashion. Garty feels relieved as his pain has returned somewhat.

"I appreciate that, Roma," Garty replies.

He heads over to Janda's caravan.

"I believe they are about four miles west of here," says Janda. "They will need a trade," she adds. "If the young person is alive?"

Garty experiences a stabbing pain in his chest! *Why would they hurt such a gentle soul,* he wonders? His anger is returning and his pain forgotten for a moment.

"We must take a chance. I have a purse," he suggests. How sad if the money collected at Scatt would now be a ransom for the young woman who carried the money to him? *If it is necessary, I am prepared to give all the gold for her life, a small price,* he reckons.

"This is the plan, Knight Commander," says Janda. "We will take our arms with us and come in two group.

Janda discusses her plan and assures them all it will work brilliantly. She includes tactics to use from several directions in order to secure success. Garty listens attentively. His own plan was a similar one, but of course he can only approach from one angle if he is alone. It is better with more people. He agrees to join in with the gypsy band. He feels a surge of gratefulness towards this tribe. *They have turned over a new leaf,* he reckons happily.

Crystalina comes out of the caravan and Garty is shocked at her appearance. Her face is decorated with gold and silver markings. Her hair piled high on her head, kept by golden bands. Her dress is full and flowing in skirts of red, gold and white satin. She has a gold chiffon veil over her face, flowing over shoulders. Her lips are painted scarlet and her eyes like pools of deep water surrounded by fish. He can scarcely take his eyes away from her.

"Are you coming with us?" He asks, as his heart thumps rapidly inside his jacket. She looks at him haughtily as if he is a worm.

He cringes.

"Of course," she replies, holding her hand out for his aid in stepping off the caravan ramp.

Garty takes her hand as she floats to the ground, like an angel landing from Heaven.

"You are exquisite," he cannot help saying to her. She looks at him through her golden veil and her eyes melt his heart and soul in a moment.

Janda strides to the pair and hands Garty wearable items.

"You must put these on, so that they do not identify you!"

Garty takes the brown felt hat, gaily coloured scarf and heavily ornate necklace from her hands. He puts them on his body as instructed.

She also uses glistening paint to put clan markings on his face. He sees that it is a good idea. He looks like a different person in Janda's shiny brass hand held mirror.

"Put the scarf over your face once we meet them," says Janda as she notices Garty tying the scarf behind his neck.

"Of course," he replies.

I should never disobey Janda, he muses. *She was right too, indeed! Even my own family would not recognise me now!*

Shortly, the gypsy tribe ride on fine steeds of all colours, including Brill, heading towards the campsite of the bandits. He hopes and prays that Janda has her directions correct, but he feels at peace about their discussion and plan. They ride in two groups, Garty, Crystalina and Janda in front, followed by the male gypsies riding on their own horses, keeping well behind and out of sight at 80 yards or so distance.

All horses are decorated with gold and silver ornaments and impress Garty well. His own horse has its mane groomed to a full shine and plaited tail, interwoven with golden thread.

"You never looked so good," Garty says to his horse, Brill.

Janda looks at him and smiles.

Garty noticed that all her front teeth are purest gold.

"I do my best and scrub up well," Janda says with her golden smile. She pulls her black veil over her face. Her long black silk dress is magnificent and creates a magical form that may be described as regal. She rides a smaller horse, a bay, with her gown flowing almost to the ground.

Her bay horse, Gale, is keen to try and attract Brill. Garty keeps Brill on a straight track and Janda nudges and rebukes her horse, too, so they enjoy harmony as they ride neck and neck.

The three of them appear rather royal with their fine steeds dressed for the occasion. Garty concludes that *the females looked splendid in their lavish garments and thus would bring attention to themselves. Their plan may work,* thinks Garty, *holding his rifle near his thigh. The gypsies have plenty of weapons* and he is appreciative of their generosity in giving him a rifle for protection.

Leading the way, Crystalina raises her hand as they come near to a clump of trees and the aroma of burning firewood. She looks back at Garty and gives her signal. Singing at the top of her flawless voice, they are soon surrounded by a horde of men who scurry from their hiding places with gnarled voices and their weapons of rifles, guns, swords and spears.

"Whither goest thou?" said one man, whom Garty recognises as Black Mack, the man who tried to harm him. Garty covers his face.

I do not wish to be recognised by this thug.

Black Mack sports a rifle that he raises to his shoulder and keeps by him as his words spill out. "What have we got here?" He asks.

"We are off to a celebration of our tribe," says Crystalina in a cool, clear voice. She seems unfazed by this dreadful character with his deep voice and wild eyes. "And we wish to pass through," she replies in defiance.

Surprisingly, Black Mack puts his rifle down and smiles at her, twisting his moustache as he speaks. "We were enjoying breakfast when you came upon us. You are welcome to join us," he comments in a hospitable manner.

Without looking at her mother or Garty, Cyrstalina accepts the invitation immediately.

"We would like that," she replies, as Black Mack bows to her and welcomes her with a sweeping gesture of his arm.

"We also welcome your companions," Black Mack adds, "especially the fortune teller," he says with a gleeful look at Janda.

Garty gasps! *So, they know who Janda is and probably Crystalina as well? Why were they so welcoming, except to rob and steal, which is a forte of theirs,* he muses?

Keeping his face low, he follows behind Janda. Black Mack does not recognise him, as he is wearing such ordinary clothes and had a gypsy's scarf over his mouth and nose.

In his disguise, Garty thought, *I am indistinguishable from any gypsy male, hopefully!*

A panic sweeps over him for a moment as he recalls the beating this horde gave him only nineteen days ago! He needs to calm down by breathing deeply to resist galloping away into the distance. He holds his ground as Black Mack looks into his face. He looks twice at Brill, but then gives his rump a whack, which sends Brill rearing for a moment.

"Steady on," Garty says softly to calm the horse, patting his neck.

They are in the midst of the camp already and meet up with the other two thugs immediately as they sit on logs chomping on their meal. At first they ignored the visitors as their food is more interesting to them.

Garty and Janda trot on horseback to observe evidence of any captive. They notice the thugs have set up a tepee style of tent on the edge of the campground. Another tent is set a little further away with its flap on the front closed. Their horses are tied up near a large sycamore tree and their buggy is nearby. Ropes with garments are strewn from tree to tree and make good hiding places for anything covert.

Janda and Garty nod to each other as they find a clearing for dismount.

Barley Rock gets up first, wiping his face with his arm. He noticed Crystalina and comes towards her.

"You must be a princess?" he says, offering to lift her from the white horse. Crystalina sends Garty a mocking glance and he understands her body language clearly. She slid off the horse and into Barley Rock's arms, turning her face towards his and mesmerising him blatantly. He cannot take his eyes from her face and just stares until Black Mack comes striding towards him.

"Get the lady a drink, fool," he bellows.

"Sure, like a drink lady?" He asks Crystalina in the sweetest of voices. "Rum or wine?"

"Wine," says Crystalina.

"Wine for the princess," he says, now noticing Janda.

Barley Rock strides to Janda and offers assistance as she releases the reins and slides to the ground. He catches her unexpectedly around the waist and she lets out a yelp of surprise, throwing back her head and smiling at the thug's gory face. He holds her aloft for a moment of glory.

Chapter 25

Garty wonders if this plan will ever work? The ladies seem smitten by these thugs, who are now acting like real gentlemen!

Garty dismounts and ties Brill loosely to a tree branch nearby. It is a coolish day and his hands are chilled by riding through the dense bush without sunlight. He longs to rush to the glowing fire and warm up. Instead, he quietly slips behind the tree and moves swiftly to the back of the camp.

If Bubba is here she will be in the far tent, it is smaller than the other tent and shut up. That is the only thing he can use as a possible clue. *Perhaps these were not the people who took her?* He ponders that thought for less than a single second. *The way in which Black Mack had looked intently at*

Brill gave me another small clue that he had met the beast before. Brill stepped away from him when he approached, another clue, adds Garty to notes in his head. Garty wanders a little through the trees and bushes and loosens his belt as a pretence of needing a toilet relief.

"Are you having a drink? Sir?" The voice of Black Mack sounds behind Garty.

"Excuse me," said Garty, buckling his loosened belt. Black Mack steps backwards a little to allow Garty a moment's privacy.

"Do I know you?" asks Black Mack, stepping forward again, peering into Garty's face. Garty shakes his head and attempts to change his dialect a little. He pulls the scarf a little more over his face as he replies.

"You too, fella!" Garty says in a humorous voice, laughing a little, mainly because he is rather nervous. The plan is fading fast!

"Love a drink, rum," he says quickly, facing towards the camp to try and direct Black Mack away. "Them feisty women are surely getting on fine with your boys!" he says, plucking a stick from a tree.

Black Mack hurries back to the camp, staying in charge of everyone, now shouting backwards at Garty, "You get back here too, or I shall be disappointed in you."

"Sure Boss, in a tick!" Garty replies, then turns away again.

I need to take a look inside the second tent and time waits for no man.

Quickly he slips past the trees and comes to the backside of the tent. He sees it is poorly made, with rips in a few places on the rear side. Looking around and then placing his eye on a torn patch, he tries to see inside where it is very dark, despite the ambience of daylight around.

Something moves inside.

"Bubba," he whispers and waits.

There is a sickening silence. He hears Black Mack and the other two jesting with the women, who are seemingly enjoying their attention.

Garty looks at the structure of the tent and sneaks out the small knife he brought with him tucked inside his boot. In one swift move he cuts the cloth on the rear side at the ripped spot. He has to find out if Bubba is alive or not?

He rips the cloth a bit more and now he sees inside. He hardly believes his eyes! There is a small person curled up in the foetal position. He doubles up and steps inside the ripped area and kneels beside her.

"Bubba," he calls out, placing his finger near her throat to find a pulse.

She is hog tied. He cuts the ropes around her wrists and feet, knotted together. *I am disgusted!* His heart fills with pain.

Her eyes pop open. She looks at him, terrified, then tears rush into her eyes!

"Garty, it's you," Bubba cries out. Her voice is weak and her throat dry.

Garty heaves a sigh of relief.

"We've come to get you," Garty says, helping her to her feet. She is weak but unharmed. "Can you walk?" He asks speedily.

"Yes," she says, but he sees that she is very weak!

"Come with me," he says as she holds his hand and they duck and weave along the tree line adjacent to the camp.

Garty knows that the gypsy men will be close right now, as they arranged, so sends her in the direction from which they are arriving.

"Go through the thicket and use this!"

He hands her a little flute to play to let the gypsies know she is freed.

"This is the sound they are waiting for," he adds. "Go."

She runs into the thicket, keeping low.

Garty returns to the camp and joins the party. The ladies are enjoying drinks with the three men, who seem to be a little merry.

"We have a long journey to take and we must not delay," says Garty through his colourful scarf-mask alias.

"Why are you wearing a mask, Sir?" Asks Black Mack, reaching out and pulling Garty's silk scarf away.

"Hey, I know you. Fellas, this joker was our recent guest," said Black Mack, taking his rifle and clicking it, raising it to his shoulder.

"Why are you here?"

"We killed him," said Barley Rock, taking his eyes off Crystalina for a moment. She quickly, smoothly reaches under her folds of silk and a pistol is in her gloved hand. Janda gives Baddy Pin a clout in his cheek that sends him spinning.

Black Mack fires his rifle into the air as the camp is invaded by six gypsy men who holler and shout as they join the fray.

Garty strikes Black Mack with his fist, and then joins the others in a fist and wrestling fight that is painful for him, but he enjoys it.

As the fight continues, Garty sees that the gypsies winning hands down. The three thugs are on the ground, groaning.

Garty slips away, taking Brill by the reins, and runs through the thicket seeking Bubba. He hears the sound of a tin flute and finds Bubba with her back to a tree, waiting.

"You have done well, Bubba!" he says. "Come on, up you get!" He helps her onto Brill's back and then mounts behind her.

Brill easily carries two persons. He encourages the beast to carry on.

"They are down for the count," Garty says, holding Bubba around her tiny waist. *She is too frail for these thugs,* he reasons.

"Now it's time to go home," he adds.

There is no point to saying goodbye to these thugs. Maybe I can get back to thank the gypsy tribe again soon, he muses.

His smile is huge, and he is very happy to see Bubba again. In the distance he hears the gypsies enjoying the fight of their lives and presumably, winning this very battle for Bubba's life.

"The first thing we must do is take you home," he says to Bubba as they raced through laneways, grasslands and through woods heavy laden with bright new leaves, giving them the coverage they need. Brill is happy to race home again with his most beloved persons, Bubba and his master Garty.

An hour later they arrive at the village of Scatt and head for the Maud Inn. To their surprise, there is a handful of women and children staring at them and waving excitedly as they ride into town.

"Something's strange here," says Bubba turning her head towards Garty.

He has an idea of what is going on and he has a sinking feeling of trouble ahead.

"First, you need a drink," says Garty, as they reach the Maud Inn.

Sliding from the beast, Garty has no need to help Bubba, who is her old agile self again, sliding effortlessly from Brill, landing expertly on the ground, natural in her dismount. The town is deserted.

"The invisible townsfolk," she whispers. "Where is everybody?" she asks finally, addressing Garty, who ties Brill at the post outside the Maud Inn.

"I might have some idea," he says as he leaps two steps at a time to the entrance of the inn. The door is open and the place deserted. Garty has a conscience moment as he remembers what the proprietor and himself had discussed and how frustrated he had become.

Mrs Bouchée wanted to help find Bubba, and is now possibly out there searching! His face turns bright pink at the thoughts of the possible consequences for him.

Then Ellie appears from the kitchen area. She carries a plate of food and almost drops it at the sight of Garty and Bubba.

"What are you doing here?" She asks them straight away, as if they are trespassing on her property.

"He set me free," says Bubba, stepping forward towards Ellie. "I was captured you know," she informs Ellie.

"I know about that. Well, everyone in town who owns a gun or horse has now ridden away searching for you. And you are right here. Why didn't you tell me…" Her voice stalls.

"Sorry Ellie, but I had to make a move quickly," says Garty.

"Is anybody else here with you?"

"Only a couple of ladies who have retired into boudoirs for a rest," she answers. "I am otherwise alone," she adds.

She puts her plate down and looks a little coyly at the man. "I am so sorry. I should have asked if you wish to dine?" she says as she wipes her hands in her apron.

"Yes, please," says Bubba quickly.

She is starving and has hardly been given anything to eat for two days.

"Right away, Sir, Miss," Ellie replies.

She leaves her own meal on the plate and hurries to the kitchen area. She shouts back to the pair. "I shall make thee sandwiches!"

"Come on, let us sit down here," says Garty, pulling out a chair for Bubba.

"But, I am a servant. I am unsure that I should sit here with the patrons," she explains her reluctance. "I do not wish to cause trouble!"

She feels as if she has caused enough trouble for now. But it was never her fault.

"You are a hero to me, and I shall add you to my friends' listing. You are entitled to eat, at the least!" Garty adds this vehemently! He is surprised at his own passion about this young woman's humility. This was a fine virtue that few men or women displayed readily. He knows humility is not his own virtue.

Having enjoyed a hearty meal of sandwiches and apple juice, Garty and Bubba relax for a while in the comfortable chairs provided for patrons. They are exhausted and relaxed together for an hour or so. Ellie has retired to the servants' quarters, taking her plate of food with her and bid the pair goodnight.

"You must tell me what these marauders did to you? They must be punished," Garty tells Bubba. He knows how cruel they were towards him.

She leans on the table between them and he notices her eyes, like a misty morning, with such kindness in her soft smile. When they speak she seems to be totally engrossed in his words. He is deeply moved by her attention.

He is engrossed in listening to her tale about her captors and what they tried to do to her that he does not hear the ruckus when Mrs Bouchée bustles through the door with some of the locals on her heels.

"So, you are here?" She says this in a very loud voice.

Garty looks towards the door and quickly stands to greet her.

"Please take a seat," he invites her to sit down.

"We made it here, thank Heavens!"

"Thank you, Garty," she replies, sitting down heavily and groaning.

"We were out of our minds with worry. What a night we have had!" she says rubbing her forehead briefly.

"We are deeply sorry," Bubba says, standing up and appearing at Mrs Bouchée's side.

"Can we get you a drink?" She asks amicably.

Chapter 26

Mrs Bouchée touches Bubba's hands and holds them at her ample breasts.

"You are all right, my dear?" She gazes into Bubba's eyes as her words spill out.

"I am well and happy now," Bubba says. "I shall bring you a large drink," she adds. "And a little gin perhaps?"

"Yes, my dear, you do that for me!" says Mrs Bouchée.

She watches Bubba rushing away, so quickly. "She is such a gem," she says, sighing. "We are lucky to have her here. I may promote her to manager after all this!"

"Instead of Ted?" Garty suggests, grinning at the boss lady. *He would not like that,* he muses.

"You might be right," she says contemplating the day. "He led us a merry dance today. I am not sure of his character now, a little absurd..." she says, closing her eyes with tiredness.

"Why don't you retire for the evening? It is rather late, almost midnight," Garty makes a point.

Bubba appears with a tray of drinks and fresh sandwiches.

"You eat and drink this first," she orders, smiling at Garty.

Her face is flushed. He has not seen her blush previously. He stares at her for a moment and then looks away. *This is interesting, very interesting.*

Mrs Bouchée drinks and nibbles on the sandwich. She looks thoughtfully at Garty.

"And where are you staying tonight?" She asks, as usual considering all her patrons before anything else.

"I am not sure," Garty replies. He has thought about riding back to Etty's Inn, but now that it is late, he is in a quandary.

"I can sit here, drinking and eating until sunrise tomorrow, and then proceed to Etty's!" Garty suggests, thinking his movements through.

Mrs Bouchée jumps up like a jack-rabbit and everyone around her stops moving.

"I shall not tolerate that! And if we have any more nonsense about people getting kidnapped I shall take appropriate action."

Of course, everybody knows that she has no chance of stopping the highwaymen from their evil ways, *but she has a right to speak her thoughts.*

Garty is not sure if it is safe to stay at the Maud Inn now. *I can almost swear that there is a spy here for Axemanix!*

However, he is extremely exhausted and his pain is rising slightly, so to stay here is possibly a good idea.

Of course something could happen, but there is a chance that the marauders and moles also need some sleep! Mrs Bouchée is correct again.

Before he can unravel his thoughts and make a pure decision, Mrs Bouchée interrupts his musing.

"I shall designate your old room," Mrs Bouchée declares emphatically, brushing crumbs from her coat that had fallen on its lapel as she ate.

"Ellie, where are you?" She calls out loudly.

"Coming Madam!" Ellie's voice replies from a distance.

One hour later, Garty is snoring in his old bed, set in a room of peace and plans.

Now Garty settles down to dreams of exciting adventures and danger, whilst his hand lays quietly on his knife. *It is sufficient for one night's sleep,* he deems.

He wakes up staring at a ceiling he knows well and is comforted to see the glistening chandelier staring down at him. Startled, interruption come via a loud knock on his door. Hurriedly he throws on his shirt and pulled on his pants, calling out, "In a moment," to the impatient knocker.

He rushes so much that he does not have time to fasten his shirt so it hangs open, declaring his strength within his finely shaped and honed muscular body. Despite the fact that he had been incapacitated by his recent wounds, wherein his whole chest has been shaved by the staff at Saint. Benedicts, his scars make him not appear weaker, but stronger to the naked eye. He caught a glance at his image in the glass and was impressed by his own good looks.

"Good morning, narcissist," he says to his reflection in the mirror as he hears someone's footsteps disappearing through the hall.

"Apologies," he shouts, opening the locked door. He had locked it last night, remembering the disaster he experienced recently by being locked inside the store room. He wanted control of the key this time, he had concluded.

On the corridor carpet lay a finely carved tray with piping hot coffee in a silver pitcher, cream in a tiny jug and a pile of fresh bread, ham and eggs, with freshly cut tomatoes, oranges and grapefruits.

He barely stares at the food displayed before his eyes, *a hungry man's treat*, he notes, happily. What seems of more interest is the copy of the local newspaper with a heading that has his name plastered upon it.

He picks up the delivery and closes the door behind him. He read the headlines:

"Young women called!" This is its headline.

On the line below this is an invitation:

"Competition for all young ladies to compete for the crown."

Below that was a picture of the queen.

The one I gave to the Jael's Newspaper earlier, with his own picture next to it. Below that in bold lettering:

"All contestants receive the prize of a lovely tete-a-tete with Knight Commander Garty Musdo…, funded by the man himself!"

He can barely take his eyes from the words before him.

"Tete-a-tete, funded by…," he repeats, becoming angry as he says the words.

He knows what this means!

"This is outrageous," he hears his own teeth clench and grind with anger.

"Who has ordered this?"

Before he gulps a mouthful of coffee he marches to reception to find Mrs Bouchée, holding the paper in his hand so hard that his hand is blackened by newspaper ink. She is busily serving a customer, so he waits, glaring at every part of the room with impatience. He is furious.

"Garty, what is it? Is the breakfast cold?" she asks him, as her customer is seated at one of the tables before them.

"This," he says with clenched teeth. "Do you know anything about this?" He asks as his breath almost dissipates with tension.

She stares at the headlines of the local newspaper. After reading for a few moments, she looks up at him over her blue rimmed spectacles. Her eyes are darkened by her secrets.

"What is the matter? This seems like a bright idea that somebody had. After all, it may help to end your search and bring some new folk into your life! You deserve it!"

She has taken him by surprise, twice, and now he feels as if he must succumb to her tricks.

"I cannot do this," he says at last, choosing his words. After all, she has given him a roof over his head and her sister owns The Etty Inn. *Being enemies of everyone will result in bad implications.*

"It is immoral," he says lamely.

His face is red, he feels its heat. *But, I will never in a million years stoop to such a low act as inviting young women from everywhere to tete-a-tete's! And fund it! My parents, if I had any, would be mortified,* he reasons.

"It's a new idea we had last night and 'tis a wonder it is right here on the morrow," she says licking her bright red lips and nodding to herself.

"Jael, the good printer, must have stayed up all night to get this printed."

She puts on her defiant look. "Anyway, 'tis too lat to cancel it."

She marches into the kitchen, busy as usual and he hears her singing some trite song.

"'Tis a bright new day, a day for sunrising…"

Garty turns and marches to his room and decides to eat his breakfast. The coffee is still hot, and everything tastes great as usual. But, the strange taste of a tete-a-tete with possibly hundreds of young women is a bitter pill to swallow.

The woman he has been searching for is invisible and the woman he needs is gone. Why would he need any more females than that?

He had already been to every town, seen hundreds of beautiful young women, so what could this avail? It is definitely a distraction and he is determined not to fall into this trap!

Mrs Maud Bouchée, you always have your way! But, this is the last time you will do this to me!

He resolved to obey this obsessive woman and then run far away from this place for ever.

"Now, I must find my best friend."

He strides away, leaving the tray outside his door, and finds his beloved Brill nibbling on some wild oats.

"I see you are still taking your wild oats seriously. I am too, Brill!"

He laughs at his own thoughts and shakes his head.

"Let's go for a long fast ride," he says, saddling up his horse.

He notices Bubba and Ted in the corner of his eye. They are busily loading feed troughs. This time, he ignores them. He has other things on his mind now and needs time to decide how to handle *Mrs Bouchée's night of frivolity. For that is what it should be aptly named,* he reckons. *My life and times are going down the spout speedily,* he thinks, with great anger burning inside his soul.

Garty rides hard all day long, bracing his inner man for a night he wishes to forget before it begins.

Brill responds brilliantly, living up to his name, galloping and leaping over closed gates, privet fences and racing through fields according to his master's wishes.

They finally stop at a softly flowing stream where Brill takes a drink and Garty dismounts. He pats his horses's nuzzle and comments as the soft waters gurgle around him.

"How I wish every woman responded as you do, Brill!"

The horse ignores him and continues drinking the sparkling water.

Garty finds a log to sit upon and ponder his future. If Mrs Bouchée did have her way he should be married tomorrow wearing a wife on his arm!

"Hey, Brill, that old orphanage is near here. I can just make out its absurd shape between the trees."

He must return the files he borrowed, he reminds himself. Reaching down, he sups from the fresh water stream, noticing a few minnow swimming around the bottom. The water is so clear that he can see his reflection and the reflection of a clearing sky.

Several hours of riding causes man and horse to be exhausted, so, having relaxed in a splendid place, with nature near and around him, by the afternoon he is ready to return to his fate.

His scowling face stared back at him and he retreats from this dark mirror of his soul. *How mean I appear now!* He makes a valiant decision in his own mind. He shall do his best to enjoy a tete-a-tete tonight for one reason only, he is an honourable knight.

"We shall see what happens tonight?" Garty tells his horse, who neighs and shakes its mane in response.

As he rides back towards the Maud Inn, he notices more traffic on the main roadway than is usual in this area, so diverts through the local laneways and byways, ending up on the edge of Scatt. He stops short at the sight of an eye catching monstrosity!

"Look at that, Brill!" The rider tells his horse.

Chapter 27

Before them stands a huge white marquee rising from the green field where the horses usually graze. He trots closer and sees as many men as possible needed to raise a marquee fit for a king!

They canter about the area where workers are busy hammering and fixing studs to keep this contraption in place.

"A circus may be coming to town?" He speaks absentmindedly.

Then he has another shock. A sign is standing high at the entrance to the marquee.

"Fee: One Silver Coin." And another sign alongside with the words:

"Everyone invited to find the Princess!"

He notices Mrs Bouchée bustling about, giving orders to everyone whether they like it or not!

"There ye are, Garty, well, off ye go and get yourself dolled up for the evening, Son! It will be a grand night, with a splendid guest arriving in a few hours. Your services are not required here, Knight!"

Garty looks into her face. *She is dead set determined to get her way. There is no point in arguing with such a control-driven mind!*

"Okay." Garty says as he and Brill trot back to the Maud Inn and his lonely room.

He presses the door handle and the wafting of lye soap hits his nostrils, tickling them so that he sneezes. His bath is already filled to its brim with hot water and bubbling lard that causes the niggling of his sensitive nose.

On the bed there are strewn garments he has never seen before. A velvet raven coloured jacket, with tails; black trousers and ankle length boots boasting a large gold buckles on the instep. A beautifully pressed shirt, with ruffles on the sleeves and neck lay nearby, along with a small black velvet tie.

He touches the garments as though they might disappear into space or even belong to another.

Hey, who is staying here?

Quickly he returns to reception and Ellie is bustling about cleaning the benches and talking to herself.

"Excuse me," he hears his voice speaking to her.

"Garty, you spooked me! What is it?"

She seems annoyed that he has taken her thoughts away from her musing.

"Sorry! But can you clear this matter up please? Have I got the same room or does it belong to another?" he asks, nervously.

"'Tis in your name and I fixed it for you, at her instructions," she explains, sighing moodily. Then her voice changes to become almost frantic.

"Get on with your bath! There is one hour left before it begins!" Ellie says, shaking her dusty cloth at him as if he is her smallest child.

Garty rushes to his room and begins his ablutions speedily. During the process he notices a pistol, loaded, laying in the drawer near the bed, and a sharp sword next to the wardrobe.

He dresses in the new clothes supplied and looks in the mirror with pleasure.

What a transformation? I look like a prince, not a knight!

He is still struggling with thoughts about what might happen this evening. And who is the special guest they have invited? He hopes it is not Axemanix himself? That would be disappointing. He grimaces at that thought!

He takes his scabbard gingerly and places his pistol out of sight near his left hip. He reuses his old belt to safely keep the sword in neat alignment with his left leg. As he ties the velvety ribbon at the Adam's apple of his neck, he is pleased at his own transformation, and vows to enjoy the evening no matter what happens or who turns up.

What can go wrong?

He asks the question and knows the answer already.

Everything!

People are thronging around the marquee as he rides into the grounds. There are already several buggies and horses secured at temporary hitching posts, erected for the gala occasion! There is an abundance of long grass and water troughs where the beasts graze and drink happily.

"This is a big event, Brill," Garty says as they watch the proceedings.

"Let's face the music. You can wait here," he adds, sliding smoothly from the beast.

It has been orchestrated well by a woman to be this succinct, he reminds himself, as he pats his faithful horse again.

I need luck tonight!

He ties Brill up on a new hitching post, safe and sound with his long lead. Brill neighs and looks around at his companions enjoying lush grass. He follows their lead.

Garty walks towards the entrance to the marquee and finds himself walking in harmony with others. As they reach the main entrance he finds a silver coin to place into the brass bucket, guarded by a local man with a twitch in his eye. He keeps one eye on the bucket and another roaming on the persons entering the venue.

"Thank you," Garty says, bringing a smile underneath the whiskers of the man in black.

He enters the foyer of the venue and looks around as is his usual practice in an unknown situation. He notices rows of beautiful young women waiting with their hair high, curled, piled on top, low and flowing in some cases. Everyone had one thing in common, a huge white smile and a huge colourful gown.

What a bevy of beauties?

Garty is impressed.

I should find a princess here, he thinks, and then laughs to himself.

If I cannot find a princess in so many towns over almost five years, how can one evening make a difference? He jests internally.

"There you are," the voice of Mrs Bouchée is ringing through the crowd.

He looks for her. She is dressed in her finest black gown with its pale green trims in a very flouncy number that defines her ample figure to perfection. Her flounces in black give her a more refined picture of elegance and high society ambience. She holds an elegant Spanish style fan in her hand and flicks it briskly over her emerald jewels harnessed on her neck.

They appear to be princess cut emeralds, he notes in admiration. *She has good taste.*

She leads him to a table that is in a pertinent position to see all the action.

"I kept this place just for you."

Her tone is very sweet, like saccharine, Garty thinks.

He says, "Thank you!"

He relaxes on the appropriate chair, a fine oak and velvet number with a padded seat in black. The table is set with glasses and a black tablecloth that emphasises the gold on the tankards lined up for use by its patrons.

"You must dance with every contestant," she whispers behind her fan, allowing only her eyes to appear within his view.

He leans toward her with amazement in his face. What she intends is impossible for one man!

"Madam, there are 99 females present. Should we stay all night?" he asks seriously.

"Spend one minute with each! If you spend one minute we shall be done with this tedious preliminary inquiry by perhaps 8:00 o'clock."

"What exactly do you mean with this tedious enquiry?"

"It's time to get this princess to confess and rise up," she whispers after a pregnant pause.

"I see," he replies, shaking his head. *This is simply nonsense. As if the princess is hiding under the tables!*

She continues her rhetoric without his intervention.

"Then the King shall enter," she adds in a hushed tone.

Garty's ears prick up. *What did she just say?*

"King Justice Swanfeather of Kallai?"

"The same," she replies, as her head moves from left to right, craning to see the people entering and who is already present.

"Take some apple juice to while the time," she suggests.

He is not happy by a long shot, but inhales a deep breath, pours a glass of apple juice and settles down for a fractious evening.

He takes this opportunity to check the candidates for the missing princess and finds delight in recognising someone he had been searching for recently.

"Excuse me," he says, wiping his mouth with the supplied black napkin.

Garty rises from his place and heads across the hall towards the candidates, who are chattering like flocks of birds in a tree top.

He bows before the young lady who is also distracted and gazing around. She turns her head and a large smile spreads upon her countenance.

"Garty, how nice to see you again!" she says, in an excited voice, holding her hand towards him. He gracefully accepts her gloved hand and kisses its silkiness. His eyes lock with hers in the process and they drown deeply.

"Sit by me," she says, lightly patting the empty space on the benches arranged for the young ladies to be seated. "It's quite comfortable."

He hoists the velvety tail from his jacket and sits himself down beside Joanne Weasley. In one instant, happiness rushes over him as a wave of the sea, refreshing his senses. They are together as if entwined within a bubble of charm. *Her lips appear plump and pink and her eyes are blue as sapphires,* he thinks. *Her pretty pink cheeks become as roses* while he stares into her eyes. Her hair, golden as the sun, piled high on top, falls in thick tresses onto the nape of her neck, *as bell heather in the arctic,* which he had only heard about. *Her dusky pink dress fits perfectly across her curved breasts, separated by the perfect design of her maker.*

She gazes into his translucent blue eyes and bronzed skin, with his straight white teeth and fine shaved and shining countenance.

"Dance?" He asks in a breathy voice. *She has disarmed me.*

She sighs and her face shines with happiness. His broad shoulders appear as rocks in the wilderness, coated in black velvet like a panther tracking its prey, gently twisting subtly to gain a better view of his prey.

She hears his heart thumping in tune with hers as they hold each other, and their desires meld together towards a fever pitch and possibly a crescendo! Together they float onto the wide and highly polished timber floor.

"How are you?" Garty asks Joanne.

He was distressed at her departure from the Etty and achieved no rest over her welfare until this moment.

"I was lingering until a light appeared by your presence." She says this with bubbles in her voice. Her reply fascinates him.

"I had my birthday since I danced with you!" she adds in an informative tone.

"Congratulations! We must celebrate when convenient," he replies.

He wonders how old she is but dares not ask. Before he can ask this pertinent question, she gives him his answer.

"I am now of age," she whispers. Her eyes gleam as they plummet into his soul. His heart beats as a mighty drum.

"So, your brother…"

"He is here," she whispers as they float back and forth together, entwined in their souls as stars bursting into light.

Joanne Weasley's eyes roll towards her brother's whereabouts.

Garty turns his head and sees him, seated on the far side of the marquee with a man dressed in black velvet, with a golden top hat that accentuates his wealth and importance.

"Axemanix is here," he says, inadvertently in a louder voice than before.

"Shh," Joanne whispers, drawing him towards her person. Her arms hold him close so that his demeanour might not falter.

Chapter 28

"Stay calm or he may turn in rage," she advises, trying desperately to keep smiling all the time.

The music ceases and they glide together yet apart towards Garty's table.

Garty's temple is bathed in perspiration and he wishes for the whole evening to depart immediately.

"You must sit with me at this table. We must never be afraid of evil, but conquer it," Garty says lowly.

His hand touches her elbow, steering her to his table. Joanne was wondering whether to return to her own place again with the young ladies lined up as potential princesses.

"Hello, you must be Miss Weasley," Mrs Bouchée says, by intrusion between the two friends. She peers from one to the other in blatant style.

"I hear you are good friends, you and the Knight, according to my sister?"

"Yes, that is true. Garty has been a wonderful conversationalist for me."

"That is nice news, and I hear that you have been seeking a job as a governess?"

Garty ignores the discussion being carried on by two fiesta women, deciding they were equally equip to express their personal opinions. *The conversation needs a new direction*, he thinks.

If she finds out about our night of frivolity she may ruin Joanne's reputation for ever.

"Mrs Bouchée has arranged all this," Garty says flamboyantly extending his arm in a vague motion, flaunting his frilled sleeve.

"How extraordinary, and talented you are," said Joanne sweetly to the Inn Keeper.

Mrs Bouchée smiles and her eyes twitch. She is almost without words of reply.

"How nice this young woman is, such good manners," she says, turning towards Garty, obviously giving him some kind of guardian permission.

"You must engage with so many more young ladies tonight," she says, flicking her fan and pointing towards the bevy of beautiful young women waiting to enjoy a tete a tete .

"Of course," Garty replies, excusing his presence at the table.

"I shall now leave you to your enchanting and fruitful conversation. I have a big night ahead of me!"

He rises immediately and strides across the slippery floor to ask the first damsel to dance.

After all, the music was playing and the young women were expecting him to dance. *Thanks to Joanne, I can dance,* he reminds himself.

Dressed in white cotton and lace was she, Antia, a young lady with a freckled face, plump and round, pretty. Her mousey coloured hair is stuck up in lumps by clips of sorts. She dances as if she is jumping with two feet together and it is quite a painful experience for Garty.

He asks her questions about her birthdate and her education. He stares into her face for a moment and decides that she is not in the least likely to be a member of the royal family. *She is far too young!* He thanks her and escorts her back to the bench where she gazes at him as though she has danced with a king and not a Knight Commander, an ordinary horse soldier in his own eyes.

As the music wanes, he moves to the next young maiden, who again seems to be barely fifteen. She has bright red locks woven together down her bare shoulders. Her dress literally hangs on her thin growing body and she keeps pushing the floral patterned sleeves back up to the top of her arms. Her eyes are darkest brown with flecks of gold that added lustre to her overall colouring. *She is barely a teen, he thinks.* Controlling his rising anger at *Mrs Bouchée's impertinence in bringing children to a contest for a princess.* This matter grieves his soul immensely. He escorts the girl back to her seat.

As he obediently dances with damsel after damsel the evening does fly away quickly as a bird flies over a ravine and returns, not knowing how time has disappeared in the exercise.

Finally, Garty sinks in his chair. He is in high need of a refreshment. He calls Ellie, who is walking hither and thither holding drinks. He summons her to the table.

"No free drinks after this hour. You must purchase drinks now!" she says in a sad voice.

Gladly she would have given him a drink or three.

Garty gives her a small silver coin. She quickly pours the apple juice into his silver tankard.

"I think he's here," she says suddenly leaving his table.

Trumpets blast and the entrance widens in a flurry for the king's entourage. His guards wear their livery of gold and red with buttons everywhere on their garments and golden buckles on their blackened boots. They each hold a long spear and Garty is sure they hold secondary arms underneath their hip length jackets, for he identifies the soft bulge thereabouts.

Probably pistols and knives, he thinks. I *wonder if there might be a fray later, with Axemanix and his cronies, his henchmen and soldiers at the ready on the far side of the marquee. I am pleased to see that the King has twice as many soldiers onside as Axemanix.*

Axemanix stands up and stares in anger at his brother even as Garty wonders what might happen next.

As the parade with its king passes by Garty's table, he stops and stares into Garty's face.

"I know you," he says. "Now, where have I seen you before, young man?" he asks.

Garty bows with reverence. This was a moment he had been dreading for years. Now it feels providential and inspiring to see this famous face at close range. His smile grows significantly and he finds the he needs to control it or he may gain the king's anger.

"I am Knight Commander Garty Musdo, your servant," he says in a hushed tone, drawing his lips and cheeks to severity.

The whole marquee has come to a silence that is almost stifling.

Garty's looks into the king's face, automatically noting his features as he is accustomed to doing. *Now I see clearly.*

"So, you are responsible for this occasion?"

"With the help of Madam Bouchée," Garty replies, extending his hand towards the Inn keeper. She bows her high hairdo as her feathers of gay colours tickle the king's nose. He has leaned forward to view her countenance. She steps back and looks up again into the King's face. Her face is florid. But, her smile is brilliant.

"I am overwhelmed by your presence, Highness!"

He reached out and somehow grasps her hands and holds them to his breast for a moment in order to gather his balance. He simply nods his head, then releases her taut fingers.

The king marches towards the stage set at the end of the marquee, where the band seated below, had begun a new tune, playing their brass instruments once more, inviting the king forward.

His cloak reaches from his shoulders and onto the bare floor for several yards, indicating the distance required between him and his entourage. And of course, his importance.

Garty now becomes watchful, his automatic detection antenna alerted, in case someone highjacks the king. Everyone seems stable and respectful at this moment.

Garty turns towards Ellie, who has returned to his table. As the crowd is seated again, he catches her arm.

"Ellie, did you see Bubba?" He asks. She looks quizzically at him as if he should know where Bubba is.

"She is taking care of the horses. Someone had to stay!"

"She should be here, enjoying herself," Garty says defiantly.

Ellie shrugs her shoulders and clears the table of empty utensils.

"Shall I bring more apple pies?" she asks Mrs Bouchée who is staring at the king as though he might disappear at a moment's notice. Her gloved hands are held lovingly to her lips.

Garty leans towards Joanne and whispers, "Can you come with me to find Bubba?"

She nods her head and he gets up, excusing himself and Joanne in one gesture.

"Excuse us," he says, taking her arm at the elbow and leading her towards the exit. Outside the tent of meeting, they find Brill, happily waiting for his master.

"Come on, Brill can take two, he's done it before," he says, helping Joanne onto the horse and nimbly springing up behind her. She sat side saddle because of her gown that flowed along Garty's thighs, making his heart tingle and his mind determined not to falter in his quest.

Within a few minutes they arrive at the Maud. The place seems deserted except for a few horses tied at the post and a few extra buggies parked in the back yard of the inn.

Garty heads for the servants quarters near the chicken and pig pens at the bottom of the yard. He sees a lamp burning inside the window of her meagre room. He knocks on her door, speaking gently.

"Bubba, it's Garty Musdo and Miss Weasley," Garty says loud enough for her to hear him. He hears a shuffle of feet and then the door opens.

"Hello, what do you need?" Bubba asks. She is wearing her night gown and robe, an old dusty blue robe given to her by Mrs Bouchée. Her hair is tied up under a light net used in bed.

"Sorry Bubba, I see you are ready to retire," Garty says, feeling pangs of regret immediately. "We do not mean to disturb you."

"It's okay." She steps outside of her room. "What is wrong?" She asks. "Are the animals all right?"

Garty hushes her anxiety.

"No dear friend, but we wish you to come to the marquee now. See, the animals are settled for the night, and King Justice Swanfeather has come to join in. It is a poignant moment in history not to be missed by anyone, especially young damsels!"

"Garty, I own naught to wear on such an occasion!" she says, smiling brightly, shrugging her shoulders. What can she do?

"Miss Weasley, can you think of some way to find a suitable garment?" Garty asks his companion, who held the lamp they picked up at the entrance to the inn.

"It may not be legal, but there is a shop nearby that creates gowns for young ladies. Come now, let us investigate," she says, by her actions applauding Garty's idea and her own sense of adventure.

They walk together towards the street and she stops outside a building near the cobbler.

"This one is owned by a lovely lady called Betty, who sews for a living."

Walking around the building they notice a window with fabrics displayed but no lights are seen.

"Alas, nobody is home tonight. They are probably at the Pageant!"

"Have you got a hair pin handy?" asks Garty.

Within a second two ladies hand him hair pins.

"Thank you. I shall take both," Garty says as they watch in awe.

Within a few seconds, he has the door unlocked with a twist and a spin of two pins. It is now open.

"Do you mean to say we are breaking in?" Asks Joanne.

Bubba huddles near Joanne. She is very worried about this process.

"If needs be, we had to do so," says Garty.

Chapter 29

"Do not worry ladies, for I shall compensate Miss Betty promptly on the morrow. Nobody shall be in trouble, except me!"

Garty's female companions were satisfied by his solution and relaxed.

As they enter the small rooms laden with fabrics of all sorts, and headless mannequins adorned with garments of various sorts and sizes, he decides to ask the ladies what is the best choice here.

"Which one?" asks Garty as Joanne shone the lamp over each strange and eerie figure in the night light.

"This one," says Bubba quietly, feeling so out of her depth that she wishes to end this saga before she faints.

"It is pretty," says Joanne. "But, the hemline is not finished, she adds, shining her light on the bottom of a wild cotton, lemon floral dress with white trims and stiff crinoline, causing the dress to spread out like a bell.

"But, I can fix this," says Joanne, searching for a needle and thread, located almost immediately from a box on a nearby bench.

"I knew it would be easy."

She sucks the white strand and with Bubba holding the lamp, threads it through the small needle.

After a few minutes the hem is finished.

"You must become a dressmaker now," says Garty, totally impressed by her ingenuity.

"We had to learn at college," she says flatly. "Every girl needs to know these things, except princesses," she says wryly.

"Try it on, Bubba," she said to the scantily clad younger woman.

The two women disappear behind a screen standing in the middle of the room, whilst Garty keeps a lookout in case anyone spots their lamp through the window. After all, they have broken in and are stealing a dress, if it happens to fit Bubba.

Garty is determined that Bubba must be at the Ball. In a way he imagines himself as a fairy Godfather for her and Joanna as her Godmother. He listens as the tone of excitement rises behind the forbidden screen. That makes him feel happy.

"Garty, what do you think?" Joanne asks. Garty turns around and despite the lack of light he sees that the dress fits Bubba to perfection.

"Very stylish," says Garty, nodding his head in approval.

"I used the pins to beautify her hair too," says Joanne.

"I like it very much," says Bubba.

They find a gold band to place around her crown. It has the royal effect they like.

"You look beautiful, Bubba," Garty says with sincerity. "But, what about shoes?"

Bubba had jumped into her boots and they definitely did not fit very well with the flouncy dress that made her look like a true beauty.

"Next door?" Garty suggests. He knows the cobbler's shop.

"Yes, a cobbler works there," says Joanne. "Come on, quickly."

They immediately head over that way, towards Cob's shop. Ten minutes later Bubba has new shoes on, a pair of slip on satin shoes that make her feet appear tiny.

"Sweet feet," said Garty jovially.

"Now, let's get out of here before the constabulary makes their move and we end up locked away for a month!"

Garty leads the way back to the Maud and the three of them piled onto the steed, Brill.

"He can take a trio. Two lightweights!"

The females giggle and he laughs.

"For it will be quicker. We don't want to annoy the king, or Mrs Bouchée by turning up too late. They will be watching and waiting for us soon!"

Several minutes later, the three bolt into the field where the marquee is set.

Garty's heart is beating as hard as the horses' hoofs. But, he knows that Bubba must join the throng at the celebrations. He dismounts swiftly and then takes Joanne from the horses' back, whilst Bubba slid down easily alone.

She fixes her dress flounces and Garty lifts her away from a muddy puddle that Joanne has jumped over. They are in a festive mood as they walk towards the entry point of the marquee.

"We don't want to ruin your new dress!"

Garty gives the man with a wink another coin as they pass by him and he grunts at them from a chair.

The three waltz into the venue as if they simply "took the air" to be met by Mrs Bouchée, who seems a little frazzled.

"Where on earth have you been, Garty?" she asks the tall male.

He stood taller now, defiant.

"The ladies are still waiting for you."

"We found Bubba," he replies.

Mrs Bouchée stares at them with her eyes narrowed.

"Who is looking after the animals now?" She almost spits the words out at Garty.

"They are all happily sleeping," Garty replies, calming the anxious woman.

"Fine. You look very pretty my dear," she says, suddenly noticing Bubba.

"Sit with the other young ladies as you should."

She uses the back of hand to 'shoo' her over there.

"Yes, Madam," Bubba says quietly.

Garty catches her arm and holds her firmly.

"No, Bubba, you stay here with this party, if you don't mind, Mrs Bouchée?" Garty speaks in a dominant tone.

"Certainly, Sir Musdo! Come and eat something, Bubba, for you may not have had any dinner today?"

"Thank you, Madam," says Bubba, as Garty lifts out a chair for her to sit upon.

She tucks her dress folds under her and sits promptly.

"It feels so strange to wear a dress," she notes, looking from Joanne to Garty.

"I didn't know you owned such a fine dress," Mrs Bouchée comments, noticing her attire immediately the words are spoken.

"Please, everyone, be quiet. We have announcements to make!" A voice thunders over the megaphone.

"Quiet please," Mrs Bouchée says to the three at her table.

Garty is relieved.

I would not find it an easy task to explain how we robbed the gown now worn by Bubba. But, everyone is enjoying the evening now.

He pours a glass of apple juice for Bubba, who drinks thirstily.

She smiles at Garty, her true hero.

How pretty she is, he thinks.

It was not noticeable before, but now that she is wearing a flattering gown and her hair is prettily tidied, she looks amazing.

He looks at Joanne and his heart swells with pride.

What a woman she is turning out to be! She is a prize not to be turned down in a hurry. But, there is her brother, watching now, waiting to pounce and take her away from any suitor, Garty notes.

"King Justice Swanfeather of Kallai," says the Master of Ceremonies in a big voice.

Everyone stares at the King, who rises from his position on a high backed chair, the only one Mrs Bouchée found that is elegant enough for a king.

"Good evening, citizens of Scatt and the whole of Kallai," says the king in his commanding voice.

"Tonight we will bring forth my long lost princess Miron, my daughter who was kidnapped as a baby almost twenty years ago.

"I believe Knight Commander Musdo will bring forth the missing princess, now a young damsel," he says.

Just as Garty is about to protest the king's call, a ruckus erupts at Axemanix party's table.

"Here is your princess," says Axemanix to the King.

He brought forth a figure hidden within a veil. Everyone stares at this amazing person, who had been quietly biding time. Nobody had noticed this figure with a veil over her whole body. The tent of meeting became so quiet one could hear a pin dropping.

Garty cringes. *What is Axemanix up to?*

The heel of his hand hugs the butt of his pistol. He is ready to rise up.

The whole assembly looks around to see who this person may be?

With a flourish Axemanix whisks away a golden veil that was draped over the slim figure of a damsel.

She is young, with dark hair and fair complexion. Her head is bowed with shyness.

"King Justice Swanfeather, my brother, this is your Queen, Anna, your beautiful daughter, whom I fathered twenty years ago. She will now be crowned Queen of Kallai"

The king glares at his brother. His face turns bright red with rage.

Before he has a chance to speak, Garty speaks in a loud voice.

"That is not your daughter, for she is right here!" Garty says, as he rises and motions Bubba to stand forward.

"This young woman is Miron!"

Garty displays Bubba to the crowd with a flouncy of his long arm.

"Miron?" Bubba asks, standing as though she is dumbstruck.

"How can this be?" she whispers to Garty.

"I can prove it," Garty says quietly.

"Let me prove it to you, your majesty."

He stares at the king.

"This is an outrage," King Justice Swanfeather," yells Axemanix.

"This woman is your daughter, you must defect the throne of Kallai," he roars, pushing the young Anna towards the king.

"Arrest all of these men!" The king orders his guards immediately.

Before he can release his pistol, Garty is taken captive by four soldiers with arms, along with Axemanix, and taken before the king, with their hands tied behind their backs.

King Swanfeather falls down on his temporary throne and grasps the arm rests of the chair so fiercely that his fingers turn white.

Garty sees Axemanix's men cowering in the background.

Mrs Bouchée stands her ground and shelters Bubba on one side whilst Joanne stands on her left. Bubba remains stationary between the two feisty women.

Anna, the supposedly daughter of Axemanix and King Justice Swanfeather remains standing. Garty notices that she is supported by Gypsy Janda and her daughter Crystalina.

How strange! Garty thinks, wrestling with the chain they had clapped on his wrists behind his back.

The King speaks.

His voice is baritone and fills the venue to its ceiling.

"My brother, Axamanix, you are making a claim that this young woman is my daughter and therefore the next Queen of Kallai, for I am bereft of offspring. However I now find myself with two daughters and heirs. How do you plead and prove this thing?"

"Please remove these chains," says Axamanix. "You know how I have a phobia about chains," he adds, with a sad expression on his face.

"When you deliver your answer and I am satisfied."

"Yes, your majesty," he replies, staring humbly at the ground.

"Bring the girl to me," the king orders, "and I shall decide."

Janda and Chrystalina take the girl between them and walk beside her towards the king.

Garty stares at the pair with annoyance.

Chapter 30

They have betrayed me and done a double deal with Axemanix's men.

"So, you are claiming to be my daughter?" King Justice Swanfeather says, as the girl comes gingerly forward toward the king. She is dressed in a beautiful flowing white gown and her hair is dotted with hand made flowers of many colours, as a rainbow around her crown. Everyone admires this beautiful young woman and one can hear the gasps as she moves gracefully toward the king.

"What do you remember from your childhood?" the king asks her, smiling at the girl to ease her anxiety.

She turns to Janda and her eyes open wide.

She turns back to the king.

"I can barely remember anything except for my family, here with me today."

"Come closer, child," says the king. He is genuinely smitten by her demeanour, humility and beauty.

"I have a picture here of the woman they claim is your mother!"

He beckons to his assistant standing nearby. The assistant produces a framed picture to the king with his gloved hand. The king looks into the picture and then at the girl, several times. Everyone is breathless as this process continues for a few minutes that feels like an hour.

When the king spoke again there is a huge gasp in the auditorium.

"You do not look in the least like your mother. However, you are a sweet damsel and it would be wonderful to find my little girl."

He thinks his daughter may be this girl!

"Wait," says Garty. "Her mother is right here now!"

Everyone gasps. What is he saying, they wonder? Is there a ghost around here, some ask? A hubbub of voices fills the auditorium.

"Do not listen to him," Gypsy Janda shouts. "This is your child who was stolen by none other than me!"

Another gasp emits from the crowd.

"She is a liar, her daughter says so," says Garty in a clear, loud voice that rings over the hubbub.

Janda and Chrystalina argue like a pair of cats.

"Who do you think you are?" asks the king of Anna.

Anna begins to cry and cannot be consoled. Janda and Chrystalina try in vain to stop her by slapping her soundly.

"Stop that," says the king.

"Arrest these women" he adds, flicking his hand towards the two brawling women and the crying girl.

"Please, King Justice Swanfeather, this is your daughter, Miron," Garty rushes the words. "Please untie my hands and I shall prove it to you."

"Enough!" says the king.

"Please," Garty yells. "I have spent almost five years trying to find her and now she is right here! I promised I would!"

"Please listen to Knight Commander Musdo," says Joanne, dropping to her knees.

"He is a good man and an excellent detective!"

"Oh, all right then! Come here, Miss," King Swanfeather calls Bubba overt to him and Garty is released.

"Let me see. Her features are not like her mother the Queen at all!"

Everyone gasps again.

"No, Royal Highness," explains Garty. "She is not the image of her mother, but look here, she is your image," he says.

"Can someone bring a mirror for the king?" Garty asks, looking around the venue.

A mirror with a bronze handle is brought to the platform where the king sits.

The king stares into the mirror and admires his features.

The king stops looking in the mirror and he stares intently at the girl. Everyone has bated breath. He calls to his advisors nearby, asking their opinion of this woman.

They flock to Bubba and begin to compared her features in every way, head, hair, skin, nose, mouth, even eyebrows. They confer together in a huddle before they walk towards the king with their verdict.

"She is certainly your image, we concur," the spokesman says on behalf of the three men who judged the woman.

"What else is evident?"

The king asks Garty this question.

"There is more evidence. This woman has a crib," he says, pointing to Janda, "the one in which the baby was sleeping when she was stolen by marauders. These gypsies stole all the crystals from the crib and left the child at an orphanage. I have details about the day she was abandoned. Later on, Miron was fostered by Mrs Bouchée, who has been as a mother to her for years now, until this day!"

Garty gushes out his information gleaned over the years of investigation.

"It was a lie," Janda shouts.

Axemanix growls with fury and grabs Anna by her arm ferociously.

Anna screams.

"This is the princess, she is your own blood by your own adulterous wife, the queen," Axemanix shouts vehemently.

"Take that man away," says the king, tossing his head high and pointing to exit.

"Lock him up until he is sober," he adds.

Axemanix growls again.

"I should be king, not this man. He is a fraud," Axemanix yells until he is taken out of hearing range.

Garty is surrounded by women.

Janda argues with Christina and Joanne, insisting that this girl Anna is the princess. Joanne stands by Garty and Mrs Bouchée is hovering nearby, shaking her head in disbelief.

"Your Majesty, what about your daughter, Princess Miron?" Garty asks. "Do you believe she is the invisible princess?"

"I certainly do, young man. You have done well to find her for me. I shall give thee a generous reward," King Swanfeather says happily.

He has no doubts. We are right. Bubba is his daughter.

Then he turns to Miron, his long lost daughter.

"My beloved daughter, you can ride in my carriage," King Swanfeather says, holding out his hand in friendship to the young woman they called the Strapper.

The new Princess Miron looks shyly at her father, the King, smiles and makes a request.

"Majesty, if you will, I need to return to the animals to ensure their safety. May I stay for one more evening? Mrs Bouchée will not cope with all the chores alone."

King Justice Swanfeather almost swoons from his chair at this request.

How can a slip of a girl speak to him like that? Then he remembers something from the past.

"You are just like your mother, Queen Bianco, who challenged me daily and I adored her!"

He is clearly now emotional as memories of his beloved wife return to mind.

He pulls Miron towards him and hugs her.

"Father, Majesty, thank you," she says at last, looking into her father's face. They know at that moment everything Garty says is the truth.

She is truly a princess. For almost twenty years she had been invisible but now she can be seen by all.

"I shall see you when you are able to come to the royal house of Justice Swanfeather!" He says this as a statement and not a command.

"I dearly look forward to your company."

"I will be as quick as possible," says Miron.

Tears well in her eyes and she knows that at long last she is someone, not just the orphan girl or the strapper who loves horses! She is a princess by birth and soon to be crowned Queen of Kallai.

The king and his entourage depart the marquee and the crowd disperses gradually.

"We will take this down on the morrow," says Mrs Bouchée clapping her hands and sighing heavily. She has never been so close to royalty in her entire life and now to find that one of her foster children is a princess makes her weak at the knees.

"We must all enjoy a good rest tonight."

She turns to Garty.

"Garty, you are welcome to stay at the inn, also Miss Weasley. I am sure we can find suitable accommodation for you in my establishment."

"Thank you, Mrs Bouchée," Garty and Joanne say simultaneously.

Joanne looks at Garty. She is truly smitten by his gallantry and genius in finding the princess. And to think she had the pleasure of robbing a shop to dress the princess tonight? It makes her smile softly. She is tempted to giggle.

Garty looks at this beautiful woman before him and his heart melts. He could not be happier.

"What about your brother?" he asks, looking around the hall! But, there was no sight or sign of him anywhere!

"He has gone with his friends. I am afraid he has been drinking a lot tonight and shall be in a foul mood! I am quite tired and shall enjoy a restful night. However, I did not bring any nightwear with me, or change of clothes?"

"I am sure Mrs Bouchée will find something suitable for you to wear tonight and tomorrow, when I shall take thee home, if you will?"

"Thank you, Garty. That is something I shall enjoy. I accept with all my heart!"

Garty's heart beat so fast that he needed to take a deep breath.

"Now, how are we traveling to the Maud?"

"The ladies may come in my carriage, which is right outside, and we shall see you back at the inn." Mrs Bouchée speaks gaily to Garty. "You are dismissed for now, Knight."

Garty is disappointed.

He longs to take Joanne in his arms on the horse and feel her warmth next to his manly body.

"That's wonderful, Mrs Bouchée," Joanne replies sweetly.

"It shall save my slippers and Bubba's, I mean Princess Miron's fine shoes," she says, glancing at Miron's satin shoes peeping from underneath her fine floral dress.

As the ladies settle into Mrs Bouchée's luxurious coach, with its private driver, rarely used and sparkling with style, plump cushions and a tiny curtained window, Garty leaps on his steed and decides to head through the back lanes in order to reach the Maud before they arrive, so that he may greet them again and assist them if needs be.

Everyone is too excited to sleep when they return to the Maud. Ellie is still roaming around clearing up dishes and singing as usual.

"I always knew she was a princess," she tells Garty as she encourages him to take a seat in the dining room.

"I shall get you some warm soup and hot bread to enjoy after such an adventure. Imagine meeting the king, face to face! It is wonderful!" she says, floating through the tables and setting them for the company about to invade the establishment.

Joanne and Miron sit down and relax with Garty.

They are wondering what will happen when the seamstress finds her dress missing and the cobbler notices missing shoes?

"What shall we do about the stolen things?"

The young ladies ask Garty the question.

He is lost in his own thoughts, but knows exactly what to do.

"We shall enjoy our supper tonight. Early tomorrow we shall return the stolen goods to their owners," Garty says as he sips a cup of hot chocolate with cream and chocolate swirls on top.

"I agree!" Joanne and Princess Miron answer. Their faces bloom red with embarrassment.

Chapter 31

"Maybe we should take them back tonight?" Princess Miron suggests, staring at her muddy silk slippers. "Oh, dear, these are ruined!"

"You are Princess Miron now, so why not pay the cobbler for them?" Garty suggests. "I shall lend you the money if you have none," he adds, remembering that she was a poorly paid servant until tonight, and he is not sure if royals carry money around with them anyway?

"We will all be in trouble tomorrow," Joanne says. "I hate this part, feeling guilty and knowing that we are now a band of thieves."

"Ladies, if I might take your burden. Tonight, will you bring me the items we stole and I shall return them myself tomorrow, while you two get your beauty sleep?" Garty extends his offer.

The women's eyes light up and they both nod vigourously.

"Agreed!" Says Joanne, raising her hot chocolate.

"Agreed, me too!" Princess Miron says, laughing so heartily she almost spills her drink. "Don't worry, Garty, for I am used to rising early and I shall be saying goodbye to the animals, sadly."

Her voice is suddenly sad, yet she is excited. This has been her home for three years now and she loves the job.

"Maybe Father will permit me to come back and work as a volunteer?" she says, seriously. "For I shall have lots of money then, and shall have need of nothing!" Miron roars with laughter and the others laugh with her until tears stream from their eyes.

Two hours later Garty hears a knock on his door.

Immediately he opens it.

"I brought the things you need to return!" Joanne passes over a dress and a pair of satin shoes, still muddy but dry.

"Or, should I wash them?"

"Come in," Garty says. He looks around and draws her into his room swiftly.

She is wearing a silken robe and long cotton nightie with tiny buds embroidered on it and a loose tie on her delicate, porcelain neck, compliments of Mrs Bouchée's spare horde of clothing for all shapes and sizes, left behind over the years of her establishment.

Garty is ready for bed, wearing his open necked shirt and pale long johns. His face glows when he sees his lovely friend. They look into each other's eyes and their lips touch each others in sweet kisses that they never wish to end. Garty has never felt so powerful or happy in his entire life.

Joanne has never felt so beautiful and totally loved by such a handsome and courageous man.

"My Garty," Joanne mumbles as she drinks deeply of his deep kisses and he loses his mind in her soft passionate lips.

"My Joanne, my beautiful princess," Garty moans in ecstasy.

The End

Author Biography

Irish-born Australian Author, Marie Seltenrych loves to design and create exciting stories, set in wondrous places. This title was fully crafted during Covid 19 lockdown in April - July, 2020, where she relaxed in her own world of characters, time and space, doing research and adding her own vibrant imagination into the mix to bring you unforgettable characters such as Garty Musdo and Crystalina, who bring life into another dimension.

With the reader at her heart, Marie has loved creating stories since she was a young girl, story telling at Primary School and at bed time in her home.

Marie lives with her husband of many years in Margate Queensland and loves to hug her grand children and spoil her cats with smothering love and hot water bottles in cat beds.

Other books by this author:

Five Golden Rings A Diamond

Runaway Princesses (various sub titles)

The Gum Tree Gang (Chapter Books)

KKMT (Version of Gum Tree Gang Books)

Devotionals (adults)

Quick Sermons (Studies)

Prophecy (Biblical)

Plays (Biblical)

Non fiction: Self Help Title:

Publishing with Online Publishers

Marie has also illustrated and created characters for books published on behalf of best friend Helen Keane (Ireland)

Acknowledgements and Gratitude

Thanks to pixabay.com Images online for images used in creating the cover.

Thanks to pexels.com for images used in creating over.

Cover created by: Runaway Princesses Books © 2020

Bookerly © font used in this edition

www.ingramcontent.com/pod-product-compliance
Lightning Source LLC
Chambersburg PA
CBHW051434260626
47162CB00001B/93